D1631240

SUBMERGENCE

ALSO BY J. M. LEDGARD

Giraffe

SUBMERGENCE

J. M. LEDGARD

JONATHAN CAPE
LONDON

Published by Jonathan Cape 2011

2 4 6 8 10 9 7 5 3 1

Copyright © J. M. Ledgard 2011

First published in Great Britain in 2011 by
Jonathan Cape
Random House, 20 Vauxhall Bridge Road,
London SW1V 2SA

www.randomhouse.co.uk

Addresses for companies within The Random House Group Limited can be found at:
www.randomhouse.co.uk/offices.htm

The Random House Group Limited Reg. No. 954009

A CIP catalogue record for this book
is available from the British Library

ISBN 9780224091374

The Random House Group Limited supports The Forest Stewardship Council® (FSC®),
the leading international forest certification organisation. All our titles that are printed
on Greenpeace approved FSC® certified paper carry the FSC® logo. Our paper procurement
policy can be found at: www.randomhouse.co.uk/environment

Typeset in Poliphilus by Palimpsest Book Production Limited
Falkirk, Stirlingshire
Printed and bound in Great Britain by
CPI Mackays, Chatham, Kent ME5 8TD

for Hamish Tadeáš

Descendit as inferna: that is to say he discended down beneth into the lowe places. In stede of which low places ye english tongu hathe euer vsed thys word hel.

Thomas More

SUBMERGENCE

It was a bathroom in an unfinished house in Somalia in the year 2012. There was a hole in the wall where the water pipe was meant to come in and the floor sloped away to a drain where the suds were meant to flow from a shower along a trench to the dirt outside. In some future time, the shower might be fitted. In some future time, it might become an incidental place. But it was not so for him. For him, it was a very dark and specific place.

He kept to the corners of the room where the noxious smells and creatures did not so often reach. The floor was sandy concrete. It broke apart when he scratched it. He urinated and shat wetly into a pit that was covered with a piece of cardboard. He tried to be careful, but the cardboard became smeared and spattered, thick with flies and beetles.

The trench dominated the room. He pushed it away. Still, it took control of him. The shallow slope, so shallow, yet running away towards the light . . .

He saw himself shot through the head, falling, one foot kicking away the cardboard, opening the pit, legs dangling over the defile, his chest and head on the trench, his blood flowing down it, congealing along the length of it.

It was Stygian and the world outside was fire. He thought that Kismayo had spun too close to the sun. The water pipe hole blazed in his mind. He slipped one arm through the drain hole and held it there until the skin burned and then did the same with the other arm.

His captors put food into the room every morning. Sometimes it touched the marks on the cardboard. He opened up a fruit with his thumb. In the centre of it was a grey pulp of eggs. He carried it to the drain hole and saw a maggot pushing out through the eggs. It crawled onto his index finger. It was white, with a black snout. It made him think of the white-and-black-chequered headscarves of the fighters. He lifted it to his mouth and ate it.

His sense of imprisonment was violent in the mornings. He could hear the Indian Ocean close by and the sound of it made him think of the holidays and work trips he had taken on the Kenyan coast, waking in an old-fashioned hotel with chipped toilet basins and dripping air-conditioning units; swimming lengths of butterfly in a long warm pool until his arms could no longer pass over his shoulders, running the hotel beach past limbering beach boys, all the way to the rocks, floating in the shallows there, then walking slowly back to the hotel, luxuriating in the still air that comes in the tropics at dawn, when there is not a breath of wind to stir the palm fronds and the terns hover in place. He sat in his corner and relived the icy showers that had followed, how he had taken a pressed linen shirt from the wardrobe, paid the bell captain in shilling coins for the *Daily Nation* and *Standard* newspapers, and sat down on the veranda to a breakfast of papaya and scrambled eggs, toast and Kenyan tea.

He sweated through the T-shirt they had given him. It said 'Biggie Burgers' and sagged with his dampness and grease and dirt. He scratched at the floor, made shapes in it, narratives, and then scored his own body.

One night a rat ran up the trench from the drain hole. It heard him breathing in the corner and stopped. It gleamed on the cardboard and took tiny breaths of its own and ran back out into the world.

On another night the moon came through the water pipe hole – a silver ray – and he clearly remembered laying himself down to sleep in a winter forest so clean and crystalline and uninterrupted. It was a

British Army exercise in Finnmark. He looked up through the branches of a spruce and saw the moon. The snow creaked under him. He was persuaded that he could taper away again with the spruce and he thought if only there were a wind in the room the tree might bend and shed some of its snow.

When there was no moon he was sunk in the blackness Danny saw when she explored the abyssal deep. On those nights he stood himself up against the dark, one hand resting on a wall, and masturbated. He did not think of her in those minutes. He tried to do it in a way that was mechanical, focused only on touch, without face or body, silent, odourless. He wanted to pollute the room.

The essence of it is that there is another world in our world, but we have to live in this one until the latter fire heats the deep.

Of all the unlit rooms, the Kaaba in Mecca is the one that makes you think most carefully about the air inside of it. The structure is 13 metres high, and 11 by 13 metres along its sides: Kaaba, *caaba*, meaning a cube. It predates Islam. According to tradition, Abraham built it following the cardinal points of the compass. Inset in one corner is the black stone, al-Hajar-ul-Aswad, which every pilgrim yearns to kiss on his counter-clockwise way around the shrine. Its interior walls are inscribed with Koranic verses and washed with perfumes. Pagan idols stood in it for hundreds or possibly thousands of years, one idol for each day of the year, some with gentle faces, others not, but all of them smashed in the time of the Prophet Muhammad.

*

The true value of gold is that it so densely occupies space. It is the opposite of the emptiness inside the Kaaba, towards which all Muslims direct their prayers, which quite possibly resonates more than any other point on the planet.

The black stone is beyond such analysis. It was broken into pieces and worn down by kisses long ago, and is held together by a silver frame and silver wire. It is by acclamation the most precious object in the world, but it is not heavy. Analysis shows it to be desert sand melted when a meteor struck the Empty Quarter in ancient times. It is inscribed with iron and nickel and star matter and within it are yellowish and whitish hollows which save it from ever sinking. Muslims believe it was white when Allah delivered it to Adam and Eve and has since been sullied by sin. Also that it was lost in Noah's flood and was found floating on the waters.

Under the floor of the Grand Mosque in Mecca, where the Kaaba stands, is a honeycomb of lava caves. It was into those caves that the religious radicals who seized the Grand Mosque in 1979 retreated. These men were convinced that the Mahdi had come to rule the last days of the world. They were fighting for him.

The caves are deep in places, with, on the walls, films of the microbial life we shall arrive at. The Mahdis put up a determined fight, broken only when the Saudi government converted French commandos to Islam. These Frenchmen oversaw the pumping in of poison gas, grenades, gunfire and flares into the caves. The Mahdi women hidden directly below the floor of the Kaaba cut the faces off their men to confound identification. Many of the Mahdis fought to the death. Those who surrendered were secretly tried and publicly beheaded in four different Saudi cities.

Being in the dark, in the heat, being so often sick, bitten by insects and rodents, with visitations of light, made his mind unsteady. There was

4

an uncertainty in him which held that the executions by axe in Tudor England and the executions with curved swords in Saudi Arabia and with a dagger in the face in Somalia resembled one another and that the blood spilled by each of them was commingled.

It was a solitary confinement. He spoke Arabic, but had no inter-preter for Somali. They had not allowed him a phone call. There was no talk of a ransom. His captors were nothing like the pirate gangs in Haradheere and Hobyo, or the Taliban factions he had worked with and against in Afghanistan who would sell any captive for money.

He ran on the spot. He performed headstands. He made a list of the books he would load onto his electronic tablet when he was freed. His name was James More and he was a descendant of Thomas More and he supposed he would read *Utopia* again. He put together all that he had learned or surmised about the group holding him, with the goal of delivering it in person at a debriefing at the Secret Intelligence Service building in London. Legoland. In this work his mind was not at all troubled. He memorised the faces of the fighters who were not Somalis, their skills and the Arabic they spoke, one to the other.

In some hostages the memory of their life before goes away, or else there is a sense of suspension, as there is during a severe hospitalisa-tion. For him, it was as if some faces were safer than others, and some memories more important. Many intimate details he could not dwell on, yet others were insistent. His subconscious was trying to make sense of a whole that was turning and guttering and shedding itself like a planet in its infancy. There were passages of thought about things he had never paid attention to, such as companies who used to advertise widely and had since disappeared. What had happened to Agfa, for example?

He wondered why it was that street kiosks in Africa had not created their own product lines. Why could you not buy a compliment from a vendor in a slum the way you bought a stick of gum or a cigarette? The smallest coin might buy a folded piece of paper with a handwritten note: *you are gentle, you are gorgeous*, or, *your future achievements will over-shadow your past achievements*.

At other times, he set his mind the task of playing back the sound and images it had stored. It helped to be patient. He put himself again in the winter forest, breathed out, and looked up. Snowflakes drifted down. Slowly, music came to him. Pop, punk, fragments of symphonies and jazz sessions. Finally, there were films and television shows, sports events; a match point, a rugby try. He became his own multimedia player, although there was nothing automated about it; it was biological, twitchings in red mud, with stanzas missing; moving pictures were fragile, they flickered, and then were gone.

The sunbeam from the water pipe hole moved across the wall during the day. He followed it. He could see it strike the wall only if he turned to face it. If he did that, he could not see it coming in. It bothered him. Every human being faced forwards. Walked forwards. Ran forwards. Looked out through socketed eyes. Time ran forwards. One day added to another. Addition and subtraction. Danny said that subtraction was the least part of mathematics because it was the taking away of what was. He banged the back of his head against the wall. Just hair. Skin on bone. He averted his eyes from the mosquitoes dancing in the light. He adjusted the cardboard. He said to himself, because of charity and love you should never allow death to rule your thoughts.

He crouched in a corner and came to terms with the volume of the room. Before, he had seen every room by the furniture and decorations in it, and by the light coming in through the windows or from electric bulbs. Here, hollowness gaped all around. The air was fouled, oily, beaded; he was sunk to the bottom, on a floor of excrement, and the ceiling was the underside of the surface of a strange sea.

Pieter Bruegel the Elder's painting *The Fall of the Rebel Angels* shows us there really is a force to subtraction: you subtract from an angel until you end up with a demon. If you download an image of the painting onto your computer, or better yet see it hanging in the Royal Museum of Arts in Antwerp, you will notice how the rebel angels fall from heaven at the top left of the canvas to hell at the bottom right. Their wings are at first subtracted for the lesser wings of bats and dragons. Towards the earth they are reduced to moths, frogs and other soft things. They are driven together by the golden angels of heaven armed with effulgent discs, lances and swords, whose task it is to sanitise our world. You will see how the rebel angels continue to change their forms as they are driven into a sea, whose opening is an obscure drainpipe. They lose their legs, wings, all hope of surfacing and become fish, squid, spawn and seeds of trees never to be planted. Underwater they continue to be subtracted from their former selves until they are at last incorporeal and see-through at the bottom.

It would be interesting to show a print of this painting to a jihadist fighter, who may never have known anything so visually imaginative, and see if he would stand aghast or applaud the angels, who spear and prick the swollen creatures.

She took a TGV from Paris and changed at a country town for a single-carriage train which rattled over seemingly narrowing tracks, and not unpleasantly – indeed, rattled in such a way that she could no longer work on her laptop, and so closed it deciding that her holiday had begun. She glanced at her fellow passengers, typecast fishermen's wives and farmer's children of a ruddy complexion, and stared out at the land. This part of France was coming to a standstill. It was the week before Christmas, the time of hard Gothic frosts and the first snow that stayed. The leaves were all blown off the trees, the streams and rills covered in thin ice and the ditch water beside the tracks frozen thick with air pockets on the underside, as though beaten out by the paws and mittens of panicked animals within. She saw the austere beauty in all of this, and the mathematics also. Suddenly, the sea presented itself between two smooth breast-shaped hills. She smiled: she was always returning to it.

Her stop was more of a halt than a station. She helped a pensioner off, then went back and took down her bag. The platform was of the kind that sloped away at both ends. In the centre was a plastic shelter like a bus stop. She stood in it out of the wind. A timetable was pasted up: there was a notice from the church, another from the cycling club, and a handwritten offer for goose liver. Graffiti had been sprayed on one side, four tags in a single colour. It was uncomplicated, but she was grateful to be standing there in the calm, not in London in the noise.

To many of her acquaintances it was not clear which country Professor Danielle Flinders belonged to, or if she was the sort of woman who would ever find space in her life for a long-term relationship. There was something obscure about Danny, they said, something hard, something striated. There was some truth in this assessment, not least the fact that, arresting as she was, she enjoyed sex on her own terms and was inclined to regard her sexual partners as to some degree disposable, like squash partners. But on the broader point of belonging, it is fairer to say that, as the youngest tenured professor at Imperial College in London with a visiting lectureship at ETH in Zurich, she was representative of those modern achievers who have lived in so many places there is none they can call home. It can be further said that any friend who thought her inconstant was no friend at all, because loyalty was one of the traits she inspired. Her mobility was not in any case a question of running away from the past, abandoning an ill-fitting childhood, being emotionally unstable, or anything like that. On the contrary, it was her parents who had set her in motion. Her father was an Australian, her mother a Martiniquan. She had brothers. It was a happy and close-knit family. She had grown up in London, on the Côte d'Azur and in Sydney, and had been formed by all these places. In her complexion and variety of dress and habits and manners there was something of her mother's Creole background. Language was important to her. She would have considered it a betrayal to choose English over French for the sake of convenience. She was broadly scientific, in the Enlightenment sense of requiring the humanities to touch upon her thinking. Her detractors must never have seen her at work, for what she lacked in rootedness she made up for in vocation. Many individuals struggle to know how to apply their minds to existence, but Danny was dedicated to a branch of maths called biomathematics. By way of abbreviation it is enough to say that she was trying to understand the pullulating life in the dark parts of the planet at a time when, up above, mankind was itself becoming a swarm and setting off in ever more artfully constructed but smaller and more mindless circles. She might have admitted that the perspective she sought to bring was too complicated and threatening to command a wide audience, but not there, on the railway platform, on the first day of her Christmas holidays.

A horse and cart entered the gravel car park behind the platform. A young man jumped down and waved. She walked out to him. He took her luggage and helped her up and arranged a blanket over her knees. His breath was milky, his cheeks pocked. She could not remember him from last year.

'We will journey slowly,' he said. 'Now. Off we go.'

She breathed in the air. It was softer, earthier. 'It's good to be back.'

'For someone else we would have sent a taxi, but the manager said, no, Madame Flinders will enjoy the cart. See, we even have the shopping in the back.'

She turned and looked. There were pheasants, a boar, sacks of coal

9

and post. They went out onto the main road. The young man held the reins loosely. She decided she knew him, she just could not remember his name. She was a regular guest at the Hotel Atlantic, arriving after the departmental Christmas party and returning to London by Eurostar on Christmas Eve. It was hardly past lunchtime, but the sky was dark. It began to sleet. A Renault with yellow headlights came at them, passed them, ploughing slush. Its wipers were moving too fast, she thought.

They turned onto a frozen rutted track between fields. The furrows were filled with snow. After some long quiet way they crossed a metalled road and past a sign bearing the hotel's name. Down they went, down a drive with sheep fenced into large meadows on either side in the English parkland style, and oaks and a drystone wall shooting into a wood like an arrow. A fog had closed in, obscuring the sea. She gave a hurrah when they came to the hotel. She got down, then hesitated. The first decision of the holiday was important. Everything in London was paid for in time, as well as money. She made do with showers in London. Here, her hands and face already numb with cold, she decided to walk to the beach. She would check in on her return, then go to her room and run a hot bath. No work. No, she said to herself. After the bath she would watch a film and take an early dinner in the dining room.

'Would you take my bags in, Phillipe,' she said, remembering his name. 'I am going for a walk.'

'Shall we light the fire in your room?'

'Yes, thank you. And could I have tea' – she looked at her watch – 'in about an hour?'

'Of course, madame. We will look for you returning.'

She tied her scarf, zipped her black wax jacket to the collar and went down over the lawns to the pines. They were a spare stand of trees, prettier and more vulnerable than last year, with climate change, with storms, the salt on resin. She liked the sensation of the frost giving under her boots in the shadows. At the far side were towering dunes

10

in shades of yellow. She scrambled up them and saw the beach stretching out of sight below. It was curved, tan. There was a dark slab of rock in the centre of it which she adored. She ran down and walked the length of it. She thought of it as an altar, or else the lips of the beach. The edges of it cut into her wellies. I forgot that, she said to herself. She had remembered the swirling around the rock, not its sharpness – the way it sliced and defined. She took a half-step into childhood and tried to see the rock pools through childlike eyes. She saw starfish and crabs and refused to name them. Her knowledge of marine life was such that she had to be careful to block out the details: the way the saltwater leeches articulated head over tail, or the colours indicating the numberless microbial lives undertaken in each fold of the rock.

The sand thereabout was coarse sugar and the footsteps she made down to the sea were demerara. The water's edge was turbid and swirling with gravel and shells and seaweed. There must have been a storm. She felt the need to touch the Atlantic again. She pulled off her gloves, got down, and set her hands in it until they lost feeling. The depths of the oceans filled her working mind, but for that moment she was determined just to look at the play of wind on it and the gulls wheeling above it. She had come to see the sea, not the ocean.

A log fire blazed in the reception. An ancient computer with an apricot badge sat unused behind the desk like a piece of treasure, a reminder of when computing machines were generously built and slow-witted and not taken for granted, and a statement of how the establishment endured through technological revolutions. A Christmas tree filled the hall beyond, decorated in the local style with dried flowers, glinting ornaments, and golden candles. She sipped clear hot tea while they conducted the formalities. She signed her name in a ledger with a fountain pen and was given a room key made of brass. A porter led her through the hall and smoking lounge to an old lift with the English word UP illuminated above the cage door. She asked to take the stairs. Her suite was at the back of the hotel on the second floor, as she had requested. There was a bedroom and a living room with a large silk Turcoman rug. It was a part of the hotel dating back to the days of the manor, the part where the ceiling beams had been soaked in milk for a year to harden them. The views were of the lawns, the pines, and the beach beyond. At night it was possible to see the lighthouse. There was a handwritten note on her bed stating that it was the third Sunday in Advent and by hotel tradition guests were invited to serve themselves lobster bisque and other foods in the hotel kitchen at no additional charge. The bisque was to be served from a blue and white Meissen bowl and the tables in the dining room set with gold cutlery. She put the note on her side table and undressed.

The bath was antique and deep. The oils provided were expensive and aromatic. Half-submerged in the scalding waters she slipped in and out of sleep. She had planned to call her mother, but lightheadedness overcame her. She fell asleep on the bed in her bathrobe and woke to the dark and the steady burning fire. She turned on a light, attended her hair, and pulled on a dress. Before she could zip it up, she changed her mind. She took off the dress, put on pyjama trousers, a T-shirt and a cashmere sweater. She called room service and ordered the bisque, a potato salad and a bottle of white wine. Her research assistant and friend, Tom Maxwell, or Thumbs, had copied several films for her. She put the disc in the player and watched *Ghostbusters*. Thumbs said she would like the Sumerian connection. When the dinner came she poured a glass of the wine and turned off the film and went and smoked a cigarette on the balcony. It had begun to snow.

There had been so many waiting places in his travelling life. His child-hood had been different. It had been settled. He had grown up in northern England, where a river flowed into the North Sea. When the tide was at its lowest it was possible to wade across the river. There was a competition. You had to hold your nerve: for a few steps you were fully underwater.

His family lived in a Regency house at the edge of the common. From his bedroom, he could descry a black mill whose sails turned only on the windiest days. They called it the satanic mill. The church-yards in the town were filled with seagulls and the air was briny when the wind blew from Denmark. If you climbed the minster in wintertime there was a view of the ice on the marshes and the North Sea raging beyond.

Horses were true for him. To ride them was not to feel confinement in any way except in the facing forwards. He had ridden horses in the school holidays across the common to the sea and along the shore. He had joined the army because of horses, but had ended up in the Parachute Regiment, not the Hussars. Still no matter how hard he tried, the memory of the touch and smell of horses eluded him. The possibility of getting up on a horse's back in the stinking Somali dark and filling the room was more fabulous to him than if one of the golden angels had appeared and he were able to touch its wings and raiment.

He was not suited to domesticity, to a narrow French apartment, a daybed to catch the afternoon sun, expensive ashtrays and tables piled with glossy magazines. He lived in a fine house in the Muthaiga district of Nairobi, but the garden was more his home. There were steps leading down to a swimming pool and a terrace with a long table where sunbirds rested and rose again to feed off the bells of hanging flowers above. The lawn sloped to a ravine. He had seeded the top part with wild grass so that it was loud with cicadas at night. The bottom part gave out into euphorbia and large spiderwebs and bare earth. It was shadowy. He hardly went down there. There was an electric fence that now and again sparked and on the other side was a stream along which the thugs of Nairobi waded at night with their fence-cutters, iron bars

13

and guns. Coils of smoke rose from the forest on the other side of the stream during the day. There was the thrum of traffic on the Thika Road. The fumes of the numberless minibuses carrying Nairobians to and from work somehow clarified the flowers and gave them the scent of vulnerability: here was a garden that might be swept away in a day.

In the rainy season he drove home late from Upper Hill past the last of the drenched commuters who were heading on foot out across the rubbish fields at the back of the central business district. He steered around the yellow spikes laid on the road at the police checkpoints. The police held umbrellas and cheap torches. The rain cascaded down, the torch shone in his face, and it was not possible to think that the policemen would drop their umbrellas to lift up their machine guns, and what of the torches?

The rain was another kind of curtain separating the rich from the poor. No one moved in the slums of Nairobi during those intensely wet and cold nights. The mud and the refuse were swept in under the tin doors. The streams surged. The thugs were up to their necks in it. When he got home he found that his housekeeper had stayed late. He always ate alone and drank by the fire and worked at a laptop on a desk by the window, or lay on a sofa and listened to music.

He liked to take a morning run after a storm down long avenues lined with jacaranda trees. He went past the Chilean residence, the Arab League, the Dutch residence, and continued on around the Muthaiga Golf Club. The greens were flooded, his trainers soaked, legs spattered, a cross-country run, hare and hounds, except there were no hounds. It was only by chance, on returning to his house after one such run, that he noticed the thugs had cut a hole in his hedge in the night. There were rags on the electric fence where they had held the wire down with sticks. For a few nights he locked the veranda. The guards closed the hole with branches and shone their torches on it. It felt like a portal.

Another morning he stepped out and found a hyena dead in a ditch by the front gate. A car had not hit it. There were no marks on it. Only in Somalia, imprisoned, did he understand that the beast's death mask told of limits and a searching for a way out or a way in. Nairobi had closed in on the hyena like the moving walls in one of those old adventure serials which crush the bit player to death.

The Atlantic is the ocean most crossed and considered by man. It covers a fifth of the globe. The land bounding it is greater than the land bounding the Pacific. Even though the Amazon and the Congo and numerous lesser rivers pour freshwater into it, the Atlantic is saltier than the other oceans. Its average depth is 3926 metres. There are gouges in its otherwise fairly even abyssal plain. The deepest of these is the 8605-metre Puerto Rico Trench. Its most striking feature is the Mid-Atlantic Ridge, extending from the Greenland Sea to the Southern Ocean. The telegraph cable laid down by Cyrus Field's Atlantic Telegraph Company in 1858 did nothing to reduce the amount of water contained in the Atlantic, but led to a narrowing of its time-space, by pulses of sound and then of light. The Atlantic shifted from a Viking vastness to a sea routinely crossed in days by steamer, then in hours by airliner.

The Hotel Atlantic, by contrast, is an ancient manor on the French Atlantic coast that was extended into a hotel by Caesar Ritz, thirteenth son of a Swiss shepherd, hotelier to kings. There is a sister hotel in the Alpes Maritimes, on the first snow-capped mountains driving up from Nice, but the Atlantic is Ritz's gem. The English spelling, Atlantic, not Atlantique, was in this case meant to simultaneously suggest pedigree and modernity. It was close to what Ritz thought the perfect country hotel should be, and stood in contrast to the belle époque style of his city hotels. It was a success: there is no need for advertising. With its traditions and quiet and remote location, the preferred booking is for more than three nights.

Even Nabokov foresaw a Jetson future of silent planes and graceful aircycles and a universal system of padded underground roads. Although, being Nabokov, being a lepidopterist, he had a floating sense of perspective. 'As to the past,' he wrote, 'I would not mind retrieving from some corners of space-time certain lost comforts, such as baggy trousers and long, deep bathtubs.'

He was full of his job and of Nairobbery. The morning commute between Muthaiga and Upper Hill had done him in. It was good to be away from it. He had flown business class on Kenya Airways from Nairobi to Paris then taken the morning train to La Roche-sur-Yon. He missed his connection in La Roche and had to wait an hour. It was bitter on the platform, while in the station waiting room it was warm. There was a wood-burning stove. The walls were hung with the heads of tiny deer. The benches were varnished. In one corner was a café with a small curved counter serving coffees, cognac, freshly made soups, stews and crème caramel. A merriment prevailed with the season. It made him sad in a way: life was so much more equable than Africa.

He boarded a country train. Its single headlight shone like the eye of a Cyclops. There was a Mercedes taxi with a sign on its roof to meet him at his destination. It was a new car with black leather seats, still with a new-car smell. An unopened packet of cigarettes sat in a tray by the gearstick. A compact disc with Koranic verses twirled from the mirror. The driver was Algerian. James struck up a conversation in Arabic. The driver turned around and rubbed his stubble and stared: it was as if the passenger had materialised in the back seat. They exited

16

the station past a kiosk, then off on smaller roads, under beeches, thence into a parkland, past other twisted tree trunks, metal railings, sheep. It was clear. He could see dunes in the distance, the sea, boats on the water, whitecaps. There was something of Biarritz, something of the Isle of Mull, the sky, the sea, and when he stepped inside the Hotel Atlantic, the quality of the tapestries, uniforms, and the attention to detail in the flowers and other arrangements reminded him of the Hotel Bernini in the Piazza Barberini in Rome.

He went directly to dinner. It was some special occasion. The guests were asked to serve themselves bisque in the hotel kitchen. He went in there. The floor was tiled with white and black diamonds. The high windows were steamed up. It was possible to sense but not to see the snow falling thickly outside. Dozens of copper-bottomed pots hung above the gas stoves. The chef in white uniform unhurriedly chopped and diced.

There were eight other guests in the dining room. Their chatter and forms were vaguely realised to him in the way the chef had been. It was his tendency to stand himself down in every safe place, to blot out what was peripheral, and recover some sense of his own self. In addition to the bisque were dishes of pheasant, goose, tripe, salted bass, vege-tables, puddings, fondants, fruit and cheeses. The tables were set with white linen, candles and gold cutlery. There were photographs of famous guests hung on the applewood panelling. Among them were Mozaffar ad-Din Shah of Persia tossing coins to the local children and Henrik Ibsen eating a goose in the Christmas of 1899. Mark Twain was photographed in the same dining room a decade later. There was the mezzo-soprano Giulietta Simionato, mouth open, chest bursting, and a colour photo of President François Mitterand in his suite in the hotel, looking out into the night at the sea bounding France.

He was restless. There was a flaw in him which urged him to catalogue rather than enjoy. He picked up a fork. See it for what it is. It is gold-plated, just that.

*

17

His room was on the third floor, facing up the hill to the parkland and the wood. When he opened the window there was the shriek of gulls. He considered asking for a larger room. Perhaps in the morning. Hotel rooms in Europe were always smaller than you hoped. You were initially disappointed, though so what, that was life, the longer you spent in the room, the more accommodating it became. What you did not like distinguished it. He had a sense that perhaps it was that tolerance of the distinctive which separated Europe from America. The United States talked about individuality, but delivered the unvaried and replicated. In his experience, American hotels were prefabricated, with piped music, airless corridors, tinted windows that would not open, circulated air that could not be shut off, a small plastic bathtub, chlorinated water – tepid, never hot – a plastic cup in a plastic wrapper. Who would drink that? Whereas in Africa there was always a bottle of water and a glass at the bedside, and there was often a hallway opening onto a garden, and there were swimming pools in the better hotels where you could swim to the moon at night, stopped only by the electric fence at the edge of the compound, and so you floated in the deep end above the mess of lights of an African city in the valley below – disordered clumps, wrongly beautiful, like a scan of a damaged brain.

Besides, there was nothing wrong with the room he had been given. It had two desks, a balcony, a fireplace, an expensive bed, a nicely arranged series of engravings of the regiment of Aquitaine. The bathroom had windows, an iron bath with lion feet and a shower whose ingenious chrome fittings had no visible pipes.

After unpacking, he went down to the bar. He ordered a large whisky. The barman – Marcel, he found out – was the chef's cousin. He was fresh-faced, but with the telltale cauliflower ears of a rugby player. He radiated a professionalism that invited candour. That made James cautious.

'You play rugby.'

'I used to.'

'What made you stop?'

'Oh, you know, I broke my neck.'

They talked for a while, about the state of France, whiskies, Kenyan rugby, then James excused himself and sat at an old table in front of a large brick fireplace. Drilled into the wall above the hearth was a large flat-screen television. It was turned off. He stared at it.

'Just for Bastille Day and sports, my friend,' said Marcel, bringing over another whisky.

He read the newspapers on his electronic tablet. He travelled light. He had one bag, no printed books, and yet dozens of volumes on the tablet: it was 2011, and the works he kept close were a few novels, poetry collections and journals recommended to him, all of them fitting onto a device lighter than a magazine. It surprised him how quickly he had been won over to electronic ink. Words were shapes. You entered them, they entered you. It was true the device ended the relationship between book and reader, but that was no matter in return for having a library to hand, and the ability to hide codes within it.

When he lay in bed later that night his tablet was bright in the otherwise unlit room. The snow fell thickly outside. Oblivious to the guests, whiteness seized the building in the darkness. There were spectres. The gulls were faintly heard through the curtainfolds. He highlighted with a sweep of his finger some 700-year-old lines of William Langland's *Piers Plowman* and stored them with another sweep in a folder on the device:

And so I went travelling far and wide, walking alone through a wild, uncultivated region, following the edges of a wood. The jubilant songbirds caused me to linger, and I lay back for a little while in a clearing, under a lime tree, listening to the delicious carolling of these birds. The cheerful sounds that came from their throats worked on me, till I drifted off to sleep there.

19

A Saturday in July in London. All the windows in her flat were thrown open. She forced herself to watch the evening news. Even at that hour there were sunbathers in the garden in the square. She took a cold shower then sat at her desk by the window with a cup of coffee and a cigarette. It was a week before her voyage to the Greenland Sea. She picked up a piece of paper that had been left in her pigeonhole at the university by her unbalanced Polish colleague, Tomaszewski.

'Thought by national poet Poland Czeslaw Milosz when Berlin Wall fall,' Tomaszewski had scrawled in a blue biro.

Then the quote, in block letters:

What will happen next? The failure of Marx's vision has created the need for another vision, not for a rejection of all visions. What remains today is the idea of responsibility (when the nineteenth-century idea of progress has died out), which works against the loneliness and indifference of an individual living in the belly of a whale.

Tomaszewski had underlined the word whale.

He recounted how they had walked hand in hand in the snow and how Danny had turned to him and explained that there were vast numbers of salp and jellies in the oceans whose vertical migrations were equivalent in scale to the birds lifting up from the dunes into space.

'On a planetary scale, birds crawl,' she said.

Utrinque Paratus. Ready for everything. That was the motto of the

Parachute Regiment. What was his orientation in space? He had leapt from planes as a paratrooper. He plunged. The air was thin. The land came up quickly. He had never found that inner space which intensified forms.

She was a mathematician and an oceanographer. She had been educated at St Paul's Girls School in London and St Andrew's University in Scotland. There had followed a stint at CalTech in Pasadena, a doctorate and lectureship at ETH, and the professorship at Imperial.

Her earliest work at ETH had been on a project to track the diving patterns of Cuvier's beaked whales in the Ligurian Sea. That had been too zoological, too macroscopic. It was the deep itself which interested her. At first, she thought she would work on modelling the conveyors which so massively circulate water between the oceans. That had proved too mechanical. Her interests became biomathematical – concentrated on the estimation of microbial life in the deepest layer, the Hadal deep.

She was a Londoner. In London, she could lead different lives on the same day. She was a star in the maths department, rich and worldly. With her parents and siblings she led a jet-setting life. Her flat was not far from the university, also in South Kensington. She wore a diving watch, a man's watch, gold, with a black dial. She liked to think it connected her with the first French Navy aquanauts. Being a woman hadn't helped her career. Glamour might have done. When she went to a cocktail party, she went to be noticed. She might wear a dress open at the back, diamond earrings, an old pair of Italian flat heels, and her purse would carry an African motif.

For a time, the abyss could be said to have tormented her. The contrast with what was at the surface and what was below perhaps heightened her natural desire for reversals. She careened between work and self-destruction. At one event at the Royal Geographical Society she noticed a man she had once met in Zurich. They left together. There were many such encounters. She went clubbing alone. It was either maths or she was on her back. When she was made a professor she withdrew, or matured. She stopped taking stimulants. She put bulk-heads in her life. She divided her work-friends from her friend-friends. Her lovers were in yet another compartment. When she went to see her nieces and nephews in Holland Park on Sundays anyone amusing might be invited to join, even the broker in bed, as long as he agreed to tea and buns and a trawl of arcades afterwards. But when it was grown-ups only everything was sealed.

Thumbs was the only work-friend to be invited into her family. Her brothers liked him, and not just because he provided an excuse for video gaming. He laughed in a way that drew people in. He was spastic, unable to contain his insecurities. His office was decorated with busty pin-ups on their knees, wet, raven-haired. To her know-ledge, he had never had a girlfriend. When she descended into blue obscenities he was left blushing and fidgeting. More than her successful brothers did, Thumbs brought out the sister in her. He was depressive, unwashed, the kind of grown man who turned around Dungeons and Dragons dice in his pocket. He could not abide exercise, except for his bike ride to work, long hair plastered under his helmet, and his summer hikes at her mountain cabin in Liguria, from where he returned leaner, and less pasty. She took meals and wine around to his flat. He provided beer, marijuana and chocolate. She brought in the research money, she had that savvy, but they shared authorship on published papers. They had a corresponding suppleness of mind. They worked together on whiteboards, alternating marker pens. They held similar views on the consilience of knowledge: it was not too grand to say that they felt they were close to a breakthrough that would forever change the understanding of the dimensions of life on earth.

*

Routine became important to her. She played in a squash ladder at the university. She swam. She had lunch in the canteen. On Thursdays she often went to the cinema with her colleagues, with dinner at the same restaurant off the Old Brompton Road beforehand. She tried to meet up with her girlfriends every week. They cooked together. There was a book club. They went to galleries and to the ballet. She answered their questions about her work, but never burdened her response with applied complex analysis or non-linear dynamics.

In love it was an old story. Her body was attracted to men her mind had no particular use for. In her experience, the bankers, especially, had no sense of proportion. One sat on a plane to New York and did not once look down at the ice and the rock over Greenland, over Cape Farewell, Uummannarsuaq, let alone the sea, and gave no consideration to her comments on the headwind, or the amount of oxygen in the air. It was not just the moneymen. It was barristers, once even a historian. They put in a hand, or a foot, and she closed the hatch on them. Perhaps it was just a male thing, the way they all seemed to think in terms of time and power. They had their chronologies – so and so did this to whom when – their instructions and name dropping. She was not unpleasant to them, not at first. It was just . . . she was charted for another place, which Cape Farewell only hinted at. She was studying life which exceeded all chronologies, which had never been studied before, and which had yet to be named. She could not imagine a career consumed by the moment. She stood in all her allure on the shoulders of giants, who had laid out science and its laws. She knew it and was cocky enough to entertain that she was going to be a giantess at the vanguard of knowl-edge, whose work would be appreciated for centuries to come.

It was a small propeller plane and they were buffeted at first by ther-mals. Ahead of them were towering storm clouds. The land below

looked ravaged, like a drained sea. The shadows in the canyons were
enormous. The storm dispersed and he fell asleep. When he woke, the
pilot was dipping down towards a coastal airstrip. It became very hot
in the cabin. They circled to clear the animals before landing. There
was dry bush as far as the eye could see and a trim of cultivated land
along the shore. The town appeared old and scattered and impoverished.
There were palm trees along the beach. The sea was dark blue. There
was a white break on the reef. It might have made for good surfing. It
was difficult to tell from that height.

He had taken the head of a Somali charity out for dinner at an Italian
restaurant in Nairobi. The proprietor sat by the door in a black shirt
buttoned to the collar. Sure enough, the menu was decorated with
pictures of Tirana, Tripoli, Asmara and Mogadishu in the time of Il
Duce: Africa was like South America in the way it nourished the
small dreams of Europeans.

He ate ravioli and drank whisky. He gave the impression that he
was a privately contracted water engineer who was determined to push
through with his work and needed a trip to the port town of Kismayo
in order to secure funding for a project there. Over dinner it was agreed
that the charity would be paid a generous consultancy in return for
facilitating his visit.

When he landed in Kismayo, he was taken to a shed that served as the
arrivals lounge and informed that the community leader who was to
host him had been summarily executed that morning for showing
sympathy to Christianity, which was the jihadist way of saying he was
spying for Ethiopia. James expressed his regret. He asked to return on
the same plane, but was beaten and cast into the darkness.

It was his fault. He had met with his counterparts from the CIA
in the food court of the Village Market shopping centre in Nairobi,
not far from the new United States Embassy. He found their comments
sweeping, without nuance, or solution. The pair said they had found

the hand of a suicide bomber in Mogadishu. 'We think it's an Arab hand, don't we, Bob.'

He took the risk because he had collected a businessman with ties to the al-Qaeda cells in Somalia. This man had agreed to supply information on foreign fighters in return for British citizenship. A passport was not on the table, but a residency permit and cash were. He had to see for himself whether the information was good.

The stakes were high: a Somali jihadist bomb-making unit was operational in the Eastleigh district of Nairobi. It was only a matter of time before they exploded a device in the Jomo Kenyatta International Airport or the United Nations Headquarters. The bigger worry in Legoland was of clean-skin Somalis – young men with nothing on their record to arouse suspicion – making it into the European Union and committing acts of terrorism there. In a confidential report to the Home Office he had recorded that possibility as 'likely to very likely'.

He squatted over the pit. He swayed. He picked apart his last trip to Addis Ababa. He had met with Ethiopian intelligence and they had warned him against travelling to Somalia. They did not know, they said, which faction was in charge in Kismayo. It was too dangerous. Why had he not paid attention to them?

He remembered meeting a standard informant by the pool at the Hilton Hotel. He had negotiated the terms of the arrangement and the secure ways the information should be passed on. They had shaken hands. He had taken a lift to his room on the executive floor. The floor-to-ceiling windows looked out over a slum on the hillside and to the office buildings on Josip Tito Road. Gum trees at the top obscured the old palace. He stood to one side of the curtain and trained his binoculars at the pool. It was built in cruciform in likeness of an Ethiopian cross. The delicate wives of Ethiopia's most powerful men swam down the cross and across it in the signature crawl of graduates of the Addis Lycée: sharp elbows, hands cupped, chest turned to reveal little breasts. Expatriate families sat at the ice-cream bar enjoying an afterschool sundae. There were Italians, Americans and a North Korean family. The informant was still sitting there. No one approached him. Rain clouds darkened the scene. The wind gusted and only the Russian mechanics who main-tained MiG jets for the Ethiopian Air Force stayed in the water. He saw two other Russians sheltering under a cabana. One wore a claret tracksuit. The other was in a white T-shirt and briefs, the better to show off his *Spetsnaz* thighs. What else?

He stood up in the unfinished bathroom. He switched off Addis. It was nothing. There was no clue, no mystery, no spy story. It always ended with the two Russians, who had nothing to do with him or with Somalia. Just another pair of Slav intimidators making their way in Africa. Yet they haunted him. Bony, with shaven skulls, cigarettes in mouths, they could be bought by any intelligence service. So why not buy them? Why not gift them national symbols, religious icons and holy water and set them loose? Why not make them Cossacks of neo-conservatism, to be called upon when everything else went wrong? He had no doubt they would kill a young jihadist, then smash his face through a windscreen.

He accepted there was little chance of escape. Somalia was not Afghanistan, where it was possible to pass as a local by growing out a beard, wearing a shalwar kameez, and speaking a few words of Dari. It was not Kipling. He could not turn his white skin black. He could not imitate the languid walk of a Somali. Even if he spoke the language, it would have been impossible for him to know all the clan histories and feuds over water or grazing for camels, which allow one Somali to pin down the identity of another in a few questions. His only luck was not to get found out: they really believed he was a water engineer.

His reports had not been read at a ministerial level. Downing Street was interested only in pirates and could not be made to see that piracy was minor. Half of Somalia needed food aid to stay alive. Hundreds of thousands of people had been driven out of the city and were camped in makeshift shelters along the road to Afgooye. Somalia needed help. If a decision was taken to abandon and contain the threat, other African countries would also be abandoned. There was no question about it, Somalia was the future. It was the canary singing for the world to hear, but no one was listening.

Che Guevara said as a young man his greatest hope had been to play rugby for Argentina. Even as a hero of the revolution, when his plane from Havana to Moscow stopped to refuel at Shannon in Ireland, he insisted on watching Munster play in Limerick, and on getting drunk with the fans. If he had worn the powder-blue and white strip of the Pumas as a scrum half, he would never have become a revolutionary and there would have been another face on the T-shirts.

When you watch international rugby, you observe movement and collision, spaces opening up and closing. But what you remember of the match, what stays with you, is the flow and clash of primary colours. Red against blue, green against white. It is painterly in that way.

He could see under the door the saturated colours of a television in a darkened room. It was like a line of lipstick. He thought of Osama bin Laden watching news in a cave, long before the mansion in Abbottabad. Somewhere primitive, elevated, in the mountains – with snow on the ground even in the summer. Osama making a point to his retinue about the news item of the day, lifting a finger, sometimes smiling, never ironic, and never able to sit through the sports report without reaching for the remote.

She liked to run in Hyde Park before work, with sweetness in the spring, laundered in the autumn with the unpolluted damp of fallen leaves, and with women going by on horseback, up and down in the saddle.

She cooked for herself in her large kitchen and enjoyed concertos or comedy quizzes on the radio while she ate. She worked until late. She sipped a glass of Australian wine while she worked, always Australian, to please her father. She smoked cigarettes, which she held away from her in the French way, as if they were leaden.

The ceilings in her flat were high, the doors were original, heavy and exact. This was her life, there was solidity to it, although with a window open to the garden and all of South Ken going softly, softly into the night, it was possible to imagine Peter Pan alighting there.

There was a bookshelf on one side of her study on which she had placed and spot-lit several Sumerian antiquities: a signet ring, a clay tablet and a pot for bringing up water from a well. On rare occasions she would take the ring out of its glass box and turn it over in her hand.

She had become fascinated with the Sumerians because the Sumerians were fascinated with the ocean. They had invented the city-state, representative government, and writing (because their heralds were heavy of mouth). Greek and Roman law were rooted in Sumerian law. It was the Sumerians who called into being the religion of the divine word, in which a god says it is so and it is so. Why were these farmers of the fertile and landlocked lands between the Euphrates and the Tigris so interested in seawater? Why was this first urban civilisation, characterised by its ability to shape land, to plough it, to build on it, so diverted by the Hadal deep?

Six millennia ago, the air god Enlil and the sea god Enki settled themselves in the pantheon of Sumerian deities. The Sumerians believed the world was something like a snow globe. Enlil kept the air in the world together with lil, a mingling atmosphere that also lent luminosity to the sun and stars embellished on the inside of the snow globe. Behind the firmament was a deep sea, and Enki's house was on the sea floor – a place called Abzu. It was a house made of colours which could not be seen, tiles of lapis lazuli, and encrustations of gems, most especially ruby and cornelian, that could not be crushed at those depths. The bowed cedar doors were hammered right with gold no brine could corrode. In this house Enki created a man. He mixed clay over the volcanic furnace, shaped it with heavy water, and swam it to the world. He breathed air into it there. The man failed. His body was weak. So was his spirit. According to the translation of Samuel Kramer of the University of Pennsylvania, the man was offered a piece of bread: 'He does not reach out for it. He can neither sit nor stand nor bend his knees.'

What is the lesson? That a man-creature created in the deep should stay there: in a house without light, without a hearth.

His family had been enriched by whaling, and when he dwelled on confinement he came back to the story of his forebear, Captain John More, who as a young man served William Scoresby in the Greenland Sea aboard the whaler *Resolution*. John was a living Jonah. This is not to say he sucked down the storm with him until the ship was becalmed, or that the good captain was a prophet punished by God. He in no way brought bad luck on his crew, but made them a fortune with his judicious mix of sober fellowship and new industrial methods. The bad luck John More had was his alone and it made him famous in his day. In the austral summer of 1828, John's whaler, *Silver Star*, chased a sperm whale through a tempest off Patagonia's Isle of Desolation. The whale entered a bay from which there was no escape. John jumped down into a whaleboat with his harpooner and two others. Just like in *Moby-Dick*, though years earlier, the whale rose up and smashed the whaleboat, throwing John and his men into the sea. The men were found. John was lost, presumed drowned. The whale was killed and brought alongside the *Silver Star*, where it floated for a day and a night as the crew mourned their captain. It was only when the whale's stomach was hoisted above the deck that one of the flensers saw it pulse. They cut it open and found John wide-eyed and coughing in the gastric juices. The whale had swallowed him. There was mucus over his body and his hands. One of his feet was partly digested where the stocking had come off. He was otherwise physically unharmed.

He went mad for a week and suffered claustrophobia. He would not sleep in his cabin, but instead laid himself down on the deck. His eyes would not focus. He repeated in his speech a groaning about the celerity of the whale in rising and its rows of white teeth. When the fog closed over the *Silver Star* he took his blankets and sealskins and climbed the mast. The madness burned off him with the sun, and what he remembered in his later life was

the fleeting hold, aye, I had on Leviathan's face, which was carved in deep cuts like them tattoos on the face of South Sea whaleman, those greasy teeth knocking me, the tunnel of a throat, aye, and of the stomach I can say it was more a tomb than was ever my mother's womb.

He lived until old age and never again wanted to be alone in small rooms or to wake in the dark. A whaler's voyage was always brightly lit. There was oil and wax enough to keep a constant lambency and there was more learning than on modern vessels. Forever after he had many lamps lit before he went to sleep. He had a ladder put through the ceiling of his bedroom in the Regency house by the North Sea and in his infirmity retreated up it to the roof whenever he felt confined.

James had no such ladder. He wished for a spermaceti candle, even if it would also show the insects, the cardboard and the trench. He was desperate for something far away. A hare. Some colour in the sky. Everything etched. The fields, the hedgerows. The hare runs into the next field, into trees, then up a hill. On and on. How it runs!

Suddenly, the door swung open.

Extreme cold enables strange things to happen. For example, at the Helsinki University of Technology's low temperature lab, in 2001, a Bose-Einstein condensate cooled near to the absolute zero of minus 273° Celsius stopped dead a beam of light travelling at 978 million kilometres per hour.

There were drifts of snow up against the walls and fences, while in other places the ground was bare and glassy as obsidian. The dunes and beach were grey with frost. Purple heather stood out and gorse. The sea was wild. A few surfers in coloured wetsuits rode the waves. She walked with her head down. It was that cold wind which searched with fingers for the rot in a jawbone. It touched a tooth she refused to have drilled. Trieste. She had visited Trieste with her parents and their guide had spoken of how the winter wind rapped at James Joyce's broken and infected teeth when he wandered the

31

seafront during his long exile in the city. The guide pronounced rapped 'rapid'.

The lighthouse stood in the distance. It was a sleeping creature, leaving no sign in the day. About it were a few villas, boarded up like wooden boats. A more modern hotel, the Ostende, stood on a promontory beyond.

A man ran past her. She watched him become smaller and smaller until he disappeared in the distance. She walked briskly in the same direction. She wanted to work up an appetite. She was determined to eat the winter menu at the hotel, which was Etruscan: golden, sweet fat of suckling pig in the afternoon; oxtail dishes, bread and wine and cake under a burnished chandelier in the evenings.

The man was running back towards her, becoming bigger, more possible. She was following his tracks and he was returning the same way. He stopped a few steps in front of her. He put his hands on his hips and breathed hard, as if coming up for air. Breath steamed calf-like from his mouth and nostrils. She caught him as he passed. He was possibly shy and she did not want to miss him.

'Good morning,' she said.

'Hello,' he said.

'You're English, aren't you?'

'Yes, you?'

'From London,' she said, in English.

He guessed who she was. He had seen her name and title when he had signed in. Professor of what?

He held out his hand. 'James More.'

She shook it. A big hand, chilled, the blood deep inside, but soft.

'Danielle . . . Danny Flinders.'

'Danny the champion of the world.'

Despite herself, despite the familiarity, she shone in that moment. For her it was simple. A hermit crab finds its shell, and is accommodated — so lovers meet.

It was before breakfast and the sky was slate, darker than the dunes, descending with the weight of the forecast snowstorms. The first words they spoke to each other were rounded and slurred by the cold.

'Only an Englishman would wear shorts in this weather,' she said.

He was more distracted. 'You're right,' he said. 'It's cold. I'm going back.'

'Shall I see you later?'

She could have said something less definite.

He smiled. 'Yes,' he said.

Then he was gone, sprinting for the cover of the pines.

She walked all the way to the Hotel Ostende and back and bumped into him when she came into the lobby. It was awkward. But then life is never neat, it is made up of doors and trapdoors. You move down baroque corridors, and even when you think you know which door to open, you still need to have the courage to choose.

'I have some work to do,' she said, hastily. 'I'm going to have breakfast in my room.'

'Lunch?' he said. He had showered and dressed. He was more winsome than he had been on the beach.

'Would one thirty be too late?'

He batted a copy of the *International Herald Tribune* against his leg. 'See you then,' he said, and was gone.

The first thing she did when she got to her room was to order breakfast. She bathed. When she came out of the bathroom the food was waiting for her on a table under a silver dome. Room service was a kind of magic.

A maid was in the doorway.

'May I make the fire, madame?'

'Please.'

Fire was important to her. It wasn't just that the snow had arrived outside, hiding the sky, making the room more precious. A fireplace was a focus. There was no focus in the abyss, not really. Enki's house had no hearth. Where magma burned in seawater it did so without colour or note. It was a volcanic heat which would burn through your craft, melt rock; it was a wellspring of life, as we shall see, but it was not fire the way fire existed at the surface; with air, the flames having shapes, volumes, and shades according to their heat.

She had the desk moved so it stood in front of the blazing logs, and not the snowstorm. She worked on equations pertaining to the speed of duplication of microbial life. Of course she worked. It was compelling, monumental. She hardly looked up when the coffee was served at the precise hour she had requested. She did not think of the man she had met on the beach and again in the reception. She jotted notes and numbers on filing cards with a fountain pen in green ink. At the end of the week she would have a stack of cards. She would arrange the cards into an order in London and when she had transcribed what was valuable from them she would shut them in a wooden drawer of the kind formerly used in libraries. Occasionally, she took a pencil and worked through calculations on large sheets of paper.

He knocked on her door a few minutes earlier than they had agreed; perhaps he was curious to see her at work. She let him in. He stood by the window, saying nothing, waiting for her to finish.

She asked him to lock the door behind them, and walked down the corridor in front of him. The carpet was soft over the boards. She felt his eyes on her. She welcomed the attention. Winter was the time to be with men. Summer days were floaty, but men were engorged, blown up with themselves and oiled. A man was more engaging in the winter, more manly and available, even if he was reduced and melancholy. There came another feeling, more significant. She felt it before she reached the staircase. Time was folded tightly, it was wadded like origami, yet she had a sense that this had happened before. More precisely, that this was meant to happen at that moment.

*

34

They took lunch in the hall of mirrors. French windows ran the length of the room. In summer they opened out onto the lawns to make a veranda. Large gilt mirrors hung from an opposing cream-coloured wall, in the centre of which was a marble fireplace. The fire roared. Candlesticks flickered on the mantle. Also on the mantle was a portrait of César Ritz and the hotel staff in the year 1900. All of Ritz's workers were milling about without show on the beach, the cooks still in their hats, the gardeners in shirts and braces; the sea caught in motion behind them, capturing the position of such a hotel in a patron's life and the lives of its staff and guests. It was best described by the tired expression a home away from home. For a few days it gave its guests a quality of life that was higher than they could expect at home, because it was pared down the way some novels were pared down.

There were so many fires burning in the hotel that day. The storm rattled the French windows. The view was bleak. It was possible to make out the pines and the dunes, but not the sea. The snow fell more thickly, furiously, covering footprints on the lawn and making pristine the land in a way that was never possible in Africa. The windows reflected the candles, larger snowflakes fell on the other side, and more logs were put on the fire. All of it came together deliciously.

How beautiful she looked, in that wintry way of new hazards. He felt he might have a place in her life, yet it was Saturday, and he would be gone by Wednesday. A waiter moved to seat them. She felt the slightest wind through the French windows on her hand like a breath.

'After you, professor,' he said, courteously.

She turned. 'How did you know that?'

'I saw your name in the register. What are you a professor of?'

'Take a guess.'

He blushed. 'Must I?'

'I'm curious.'

'Music?'

'No.'

35

'Anthropology?'

'Please.'

'Law?'

'Wrong again.'

'What then?'

'Maths. I apply mathematics to the study of life in the ocean.' She studied his expression. There was nothing of academia about him, nothing comical. Except that he was square-jawed with strong zygomatic muscles, clean-shaven, imperial somehow, with fine blood vessels on his cheekbones; when he smiled it was as if his face was illuminated.

He smiled. 'You're an oceanographer!'

She was already spreading butter on bread. She jabbed the air with her blunt knife. 'There's no such discipline as oceanography,' she said. 'It's just the working of sciences to whatever is in the sea.'

'Or under the sea.'

She looked up. It was strange he said that. 'Precisely,' she said.

'Which is your ocean?'

'Sorry?'

'Which ocean do you like the best?'

'Oh, I see. That's easy.' She gestured towards the windows. 'It has to be that one – the Atlantic.'

'Why's that?'

'Scientifically, or otherwise?'

'Otherwise, I suppose,' he said, cautiously. He sensed he was being measured.

'Well, the Atlantic links the halves of the Western world. It is the ocean of the slave trade, also of the steam ship. The sea of constant doom, the Phoenicians called it. It has the Gulf Stream. There are the colours. The greys and greens. The seabird colonies. Apart from that it's a cold and representative body of water, dropping down to submarine mountain ranges.'

'How deep?'

'An average depth of 3600 metres.'

'Mrs Memory!'

'*The 39 Steps*?'

'Like I say, Mrs Memory.'

She laughed gaily. 'What about you? What do you do?'

He answered in an instant. He did not want her to guess. 'I consult on water projects in Africa.'

'A charitable man.'

'For the British government,' he added.

'So you live in Africa?'

'In Nairobi.'

'Do you like it?'

One of the first things he had been taught in the intelligence service was how to push conversation away from the realities of the job. He did not speak to her in detail about his cover as a water consultant, only of his genuine impressions of Africa. He described to her his garden in Muthaiga – the hanging flowers, the pool, the way the tree trunks turned vermilion with ants after rain, his housekeeper, his cook, and elderly gardener. He made it clear he lived alone. Then, matching the polarity of the day, he told her a story of how he had ridden a polo pony into Nairobi's Ngong forest in the half-light and had seen a stolen car engine hoisted high in the tree, a monkey sitting on it, the ropes creaking, the metal like a nest, and he explained to her the reason there were so many hyenas in the forest.

'The poorest people in the Kibera slum can't afford a coffin, so they carry their dead into the forest at night and bury them with a short ceremony under the stump of a mugoma tree. Unthinkingly, they feed the hyenas.'

He went on to explain, as best he could, that although those doing the burying were Luos, originally from Lake Victoria, the rough treat-ment given to the pauper corpses by the hyenas was similar to a death rite of the Kikuyu, last recorded in 1970, in which a dying man or

37

woman was pushed into a grass hut the size of a hutch, with an opening at either side, one for pushing the nearly dead relative in, the other for the hyena to drag the fresh body out.

'Time is compressed there,' he said. 'Kenya has gone in a couple of centuries from some ancient and unwritten place to a hinterland for Arab traders and slavers, to a blank on a map which the white hunters explored, then, hey ho, a colony. Now it's the Republic of Kenya, a country which doubles its population every generation.'

She appeared to be fascinated. 'There must be people alive who remember the hyena death rites,' she said.

'My cook's grandmother was eaten by hyenas.'

'No!'

Emboldened, he went on to tell her it was only a generation since the death of the Danish writer Countess Blixen – Karen Blixen – in her seaside manor on the Zealand coast north of Copenhagen. She who had grandly considered her coffee estate at the edge of Nairobi as an eighteenth-century English landscape, in which there was an abundance of horses, dogs, servants – and lions – but never any money.

'The night in Nairobi is like a river,' he said.

'What do you mean?'

'It's deep and treacherous in the way of African rivers, you can't see into it, you have no idea where the crocodiles are, or where the rapids run. It has its own lustre.'

She gave nothing back to his stories. Perhaps she was just guarded. She knew nothing of development work or consultancies. It was said she was worldly. Well, she was worldly in wealth, and had been worldly enough in the toilet stalls of nightclubs, but she was not properly worldly. She had not come into contact with the poor. She was spoilt, like her mother. Her instinct was for refinement – of literature, fashion, cuisine – refinement of everything really, and what could not be refined was not worth having. Could poverty be refined? She did not think so. On her visits to Australia she headed to the galleries in Sydney. These days, Manly was seamy enough for her. She had been taken to

Flinders Island, which had been named for her paternal forebear. Despite her father's insistence, she had never visited an Aboriginal community in Australia or shown any interest in indiginous culture, except in so far as to use its images and textiles to garland her life. She was a woman with slave ancestry, yet she was prejudiced against Africa as a continent without research universities. Aside from a trip to Cape Town she had only been to Africa once, on an oceanographic research vessel that had anchored off the coast of Senegal. They had motored ashore in great excitement, but the village they arrived at had left her embarrassed. The village women gathered around her and asked her to speak on their behalf. They recognised her. She felt found out. It was not about skin colour; that was of no importance. It was a sudden sense of community, a rusticity which complicated her metropolitan identity.

That is not to say she was porcellaneous. She was rather the opposite: physically and emotionally hard to break; generous, weighted, in no way translucent. She preferred to be defined as a scientist. She felt she had contained within her an understanding of a greater polarity than that which James described between the rich and poor in Nairobi, and still larger than the contrast which existed that winter afternoon between the candlelit mirrored room in the hotel and the snows outside. What was it? It was the division between life on the surface of the world and the life she studied in the Hadal deep; light and dark, air and water, the breathing and the drowned. She almost wanted to say it was the division between the saved and the damned, but, no, that was not right.

When he coaxed her, she spoke quietly about the Hotel Atlantic. She said she had been coming to the hotel for several years.

'I even know why Asturian stew is on the menu.'

'What is it?'

'A peasant dish made of pork shoulder, sausage and beans.' She related the story the hotel manager had told her: 'A Spanish nobleman in the court of Alfonso XIII staying here before the First World War

39

challenged a Russian to a game of chess of using life-sized pieces. These two men stood on separate balconies overlooking the lawn and commanded the chess pieces, which were made up of serving girls, farm labourers, and children from the village on the other side of the wood — all dressed in costume and standing for hours on their required squares. It was in autumn. Cold. The Spaniard played white and the Russian black. They wagered large bets on the outcome and on the taking of certain pieces with certain other pieces: a knight taking a rook was worth a motor car, for example. Cider was served to the pieces. Naturally, as the afternoon wore on, a fight broke out between opposing rooks, the one running after the other, scattering the pawns, and a bishop had to intervene. The game went on late into the evening. When the pieces were taken, they were given a few francs for their trouble and a bowl of Asturian stew on the Spaniard's account to warm up.'

He had pheasant, she sole. They kept looking at each other, leaning, peering. The wind subsided and the snow fell thickly through the fog, as though it were falling underwater. The sheep moved out there in the whiteness, behind the railings. It was a winter afternoon of the old world, old Europe, weightless for Danny and James. The split logs burned on the fire with the bark on them, the resin sputtered; they imagined wolves in the wood, the paths to the outlying village and church tangled. Every breath they took drew them closer to the nativity which repeated: the Annunciation to the shepherds, the straw arranged in the manger, the smell of animals, the bleating, the star shining bright.

More wine was poured for them into crystal glasses. The tables were square and set at an angle. From the chandelier, they looked like dice. The dishes were dots denoting numbers. The guests at the other tables had their own stories, occasionally they flashed a piece of cutlery, but they were in the background; her eyes ran across them as across hypertext.

She saw him presently. She was seduced, although there was

something that was not true. The man sitting across from her, so boyishly tucking into his dessert, was concealing another history. She did not know what, she had no reference, only that the bones in his soft hands were broken, and he was scarred about the nose and the ear. There was some shutting down in him. His eyes showed it. He had been abraded by the world.

They took coffee in the bar. Another guest slotted euros into a vintage jukebox which had on it a picture of Johnny Hallyday.

They had no choice. *I believe when I fall in love with you it will be forever.* She rolled her eyes.

'Even so,' he said, and raised his cup.

She stared at him. His pupils were dilated, the effect darker. She was a little drunk.

They parted at the foot of the stairs. She went up and he went out into an afternoon that appeared to have no up or down. The snow swirled. He could not see his way forward. He heard the sheep. He thought he had arrived at the railings, but a few more steps brought him back to the hotel. All that was visible of the building was the sign over the entrance spelling out its name in light bulbs, and the green figurines of mermaids backed by dark green tiles of the highest quality purloined from a Persian mosque.

Without warning he was battered with conflicting emotions and identities, as if a train had braked hard and all the baggage had come crashing down on top of him. He took the lift up. He closed the cage door and pressed in the button. It was a rosewood box, slightly larger than a coffin. He tried not to notice the ascent. He sat in his room, staring out of the window and only occasionally shifting his focus from the blankness to the icicles hanging down. He did not draw the curtains when it got dark and allowed the maid who came to turn down his bed only to switch on a lamp and to bring him a bottle of water and a pot of hot chocolate.

She worked into the evening. She was befuddled by the alcohol, by him. Maths was like playing the piano, in a way. You had to keep practising to keep fluent and supple; eventually the discipline became a pleasure.

She turned on the television and watched a tennis match being played at the Albert Hall in London. The acoustics in the hall were such that the man's serve sounded like a detonation.

He was hauled up by his wrists and made to stand. His legs shook.

'I'll shit myself,' he said.

His bowels softened; a watery mess flowed down the inside of his thighs.

There was shouting in Somali. He was struck in the back of the head and in the face and doused in seawater. He was dragged into an alley. It was blinding. He could not look up. The sand burned and was littered with thorns and with glistening donkey droppings and palm fronds. There were wattle-and-daub shacks on either side. He heard children playing. He sensed the women stopping as he passed. He was nauseous. His head spun. He tried to concentrate on the feet of the man in front of him. He said to himself, the flip-flops are red, they are red, the calloused heel lifts, now it strikes the sand, now it lifts.

They came out into the open. The wind gusted. Crabs scuttled back to holes in the sand. When he finally raised his head and looked at the world he saw surf exploding on a reef and a monumental orange sun hovering over the Indian Ocean.

The fighters got on their knees and prayed to Mecca.

After some minutes one of them stood up. 'We will kill you now,' he said, without emotion.

They pushed him towards the sea. He saw it. They would shoot him in the water. There would be no need for a shroud.

When his body was drained they could dump it in the infidels' cemetery. With what prayer, with what damnable prayer?

The fighters were young and thin, but he was too weak to take advantage. He was a white man in a part of Somalia controlled by jihadists. Even if he cracked heads, snapped necks and took a gun, there was no place to run. So, he straightened himself and prepared to die.

But how does a man do that? Nature is pre-contracted, her demands beyond negotiation. You cannot wish yourself immortal any more than you can bid the apples come in May, or the leaves stick in October. A terminal illness at least gives you a chance to say goodbye to your family, friends and acquaintances. A violent death is something else. It is a maelstrom. Its waters turn quickly, they spiral down, the sky is blotted out and there is no time to make a phone call or take a bow.

He wanted to lay out his memories on the sand like photographs; to leave a message for the world and take a lesson from it. But he was turning, he was going down, the whaleboat was splintering, the waters were freezing. The flotsam people clung to in life, which kept them afloat in the world, were fictions found in stories. He reached for them. He recited the Lord's Prayer.

They pushed him into deeper water. It was almost up to his waist. Look how the dirt is lifting in filaments from your feet, he said to himself, the filth is lifting, and he glimpsed himself, it was difficult to describe, underwater, in a stovepipe hat, a whaler thrown overboard, sinking to the bottom, an eel roped where his intestines had been, with, in the grainy distance, a whaling vessel going down, in imitation of the slave ship Danny described, perhaps, except with a hawk nailed to its mast, the archangelic shriek silenced . . . thy will be done, in earth as it is heaven.

They took their hands off him. He looked out over the sea. Submarines go across. They keep to the shallows. There were many things he had not properly imagined. Death was one, the ocean was another. It was fitting, comforting even. The earth really was the ocean. Danny had taught him another way of looking at things, how being made of saline solution, a jelly with pin-like bones, he was yet alien to the greater part of the planet that was saltwater. He looked up. He glimpsed a gull. They lifted their weapons. He had no strength left. He hated them, and was ashamed of himself.

'*Allah u Akbar!*'

There was a burst of gunfire. He fell into the sea. The bullets went into the sky. He was on his knees in the water. He thrashed forward. He cried out and pulled off his soiled kikoi and washed himself between his legs. His tears moved the fighters. One of them waded after him and took off his own headscarf and wrapped it around him, so that he would not be naked when they carried him back to land.

She was a morning person, he was not.

His phone rang before dawn. His first waking word was a profanity. 'Yes? Who is it?'

'I'm heading down to the beach for a swim. Will you join me?'

'At this hour? In the snow?' He sat up. 'OK,' then, 'I shan't swim.'

'See you downstairs,' she said cheerfully, and rang off.

It was the first light of a clear day. The patches of ice were all covered up. The snow came up over their boots. There were boar hunters in the woods; gunshots could be heard coming from the direction of the church and the village. The pines were rimed with salt, the holly berries shone

44

blood red. On the beach the snow gave way to spindrift and then to the return of long breaking waves. He carried towels and an extra sweater. He was uncertain if she would actually swim. He did not know her travels had taken her in the opposite direction to him, that her voyages had moved her closer to the Inuit and further from the Carib.

The sand was firm. Their footsteps filled with water after them.

'This is just the place to have a dog,' he said. 'They could run for miles.'

'I don't like dogs.'

His heart sank. She was harsh. What was he doing on the beach at this hour?

When he was a boy, the family priest, an Irishman, had told him: James, there is never a moment in a life when a selfish heart is satisfied.

He wanted a country life. He wanted a cottage. He wanted a garden. He wanted gundogs and horses. Perhaps it was a feint, a way of dealing with his career. What did he need?

She caught his fallen expression. He was a spy, but utterly readable. 'Cheer up. I could learn to love a dog. Singular.'

He smiled at her. He felt they needed to hold on to one another or they would be swept apart and not find each other again. They stood and looked out over the crescent-shaped expanse of the Atlantic.

'Let's get on with it,' she said. Unexpectedly, she reached up and touched his cheek.

She moved fluently and without hesitation. She pulled off her wellington boots and socks, her fleece-lined tracksuit trousers. She wore light knickers with a darker trim. Her hips were wide. Her skin rose at once to the new day in ranges of goose pimples. She took off her wax jacket, scarf and woollen hat. She peeled off her cashmere sweater and was naked. She ran and dived into the sea. A wave crashed over her. She did not shout or call out as he expected she would. She lay herself down and stretched out between the waves. Her fists were clenched. She held onto the water. Then she kicked away in a front crawl. She was a strong swimmer, stronger than he was. She swam in line with the shore, then stood up and ran out, her feet catching on the shells and gravel. Her nipples were large and brown and pulled tight with the cold. She was youthful in the thickening of her belly, and her broad shoulders in the winter sun made her frame momentarily appear to be facets of a gem. She took off her knickers and rubbed her chest down with one towel while he rubbed her legs and hips with the other. Her hair was wet across her face. She dressed as quickly as she had undressed. She could not speak for breathing. They set off towards the hotel at a fast pace.

Without any indication it could be otherwise, he went up the stairs with her to her suite. She drew a bath. He turned on the television. When the bath was full and he heard her laying back in it he became distracted and after some minutes, as if pulled by orbital forces, he undressed and went into the bathroom and slid in with her, so the suds spilled out over the tiles. She embraced him and they lay together and then rose and he made love to her over the sink. She pushed him out and took his manhood and handed him off over her belly, up to her chest.

There was then that unforgiving moment which follows the coming before. She dreaded it. It was so often a disappointment and many times worse. She fucked and instantly deduced it had been the act only. She returned to herself, to Flinders, to the scientist. But no such rift opened between Danny and James that might have obliged them to walk separately out of the bathroom. The tiles on the floor stayed sure, affixed one to the other, and there was only tenderness between them.

They dozed hand in hand in bed. Later, she found a condom in one of her bags and peeled it onto him in a similar motion to how she had unpeeled her sweater on the beach, and they made love steadily. A while later it was more powerful. It was as if they were screwing each other to a place where the body is spent and the true affair can begin.

*

It was a morning on Christmas week and it might have been absolute zero outside, with everything slowed and congealed into superatoms. He was unconcerned with emailing Legoland. She put her work aside. They ordered sweet, buttery porridge, juice and coffee. The suite was rearranged around them, the fire lighted. For that short day they were curled together on a blue and silver embroidered sofa. They chose to watch *A Matter of Life and Death*, with David Niven in the lead. An opening sequence of the universe cut to Squadron Leader Peter Carter, his burning Lancaster bomber plane dropping into the English Channel, giving his last thoughts to June, an American radio operator:

'But at my back I always hear, Time's winged chariot hurrying near; and yonder all before us lie deserts of vast eternity.' Andy Marvell, what a marvel. What's your name?

Carter jumped from the Lancaster without a parachute, expecting to die. The next scene showed him climbing out of the sea and wandering in dunes not unlike those around the Hotel Atlantic. By fault of angels, who missed him in the pea-soup fog, Carter miracu- lously survived into a technicolour so intense, the first technicolour of British cinema, that the sofa became colourless and the wintry sky outside, which was prismatic when they sat down, cloudless, with wisps of orange, turned to gruel.

In Francis Bacon's work *New Atlantis* there is a description of perspective-houses:

where we make demonstrations of all lights and radiations; and of all colours: and out of things uncoloured and transparent, we can represent unto you all several colours; not in rainbows (as it is in gems and prisms), but of themselves single. We represent also all multiplications of light, which we carry to great distance, and make so sharp as to discern small points and lines. Also of colourations of light; all delusions and deceits of the sight, in figures, magnitudes, motions, colours all demonstrations of shadows. We find also divers means, yet unknown to you, of producing of light originally from divers bodies. We procure means of seeing objects afar off; as in heaven and remote places; and represent things near as afar off; and things afar off as near; making feigned distances. We have also help for the sight, far above spectacles and glasses in use. We have also glasses and means to see small and minute bodies perfectly and distinctly; as the shapes and colours of small flies and worms, grains and flaws in gems, which cannot otherwise be seen.

It is common knowledge that Osama bin Laden was born into a rich Saudi family. It is less known that the family fortune was invested in Western banks in contravention of Islamic law. If Osama had been born a poor Saudi, things might have been different. So would they be if he was born into a rich family in another country. If he had been an Italian industrialist's son, for example, he might have exercised his religious feeling by becoming a priest in the Order of Daniel Comboni, whose motto is *Africa or Death!*

It would not have been possible for that alternate Osama, Father Giacomo Ladini, to stray so far from the sanctity of life.

He had lain down beside the trench and had a dream so lifelike he could not believe it was his alone. It was a Lenten carnival. A Christ-like figure on a float was leading a crowd of young people in a dance. The music was techno. The street was narrow. Bodies were pressed up against old buildings. There were shouts in German and French. It might have been the pharmaceutical town of Basel. The Christ spelled out a message in hand movements like the hand movements of the flagellants who marched through Rhineland towns during the Black Death spelling out *I am a liar, a thief, an adulterer,* except that these hand movements were not confessional: the Christ and the crowd repeated over and over with their hands a thousand years of love, a thousand years of peace.

The faces were diverse. They were moved by a common happiness. Then there was a pop of a suicide bomber's vest, a drawing in of air, and an exhaling, so that the carnival float, the Christ, and many in the crowd were reduced to shreds.

They carried him from the sea to a whitewashed mosque separated from the beach by a wall of coral and lava stone. It was an old mosque; the first believers in Kismayo were buried in a shrine in the courtyard. The doors and window frames were intricately carved from planks of mango wood.

They put him on a cement floor in a smoke-blackened room at the back of the mosque. He was nauseous. There was ringing in his ears. A pile of mobile phones on a carpet vibrated, stirring motes of fecal dust and frankincense in light that slanted down from windows which were barred but held no glass. His vision blurred. When he came to a lantern cast the same room more richly, so at first sight the faces of the commander and the fighters were like those in a Netherlandish painting.

The commander was sitting cross-legged on the carpet. He recognised him as Yusuf Mohamud al-Afghani, a forward commander of

49

al-Qaeda in Somalia: thickset for a Somali, but with the usual Somali vanity, the hair crimped and made to shine like a songbird, like a jazz singer, the beard short and smoothed with ointments and dyed with henna, so that its underside was ginger.

Hair was the quality of the Pakistanis sat on either side of Yusuf: it curled and spilled astrakhan-like from their faces and shoulders and down their forearms and wrists and knuckles and piled in a greasy sheen under their headscarves.

He counted a dozen others in the room, most were Somali boys with very white teeth. Kalashnikovs and grenade launchers were stacked against one wall, sacks of frankincense piled high against another. Some of the men sat on crates of ammunition. A cheap Chinese clock with a picture of the Grand Mosque in Mecca on its dial hung over the door.

On the wall behind Yusuf was a framed page of the Koran, a newspaper cutting of Osama bin Laden before his submergence, and a poster of the French footballer Thierry Henry playing for Arsenal. There were rat droppings. There was litter. A teakettle simmered on a low paraffin flame in the centre. Beside it were bowls, a pot of steaming rice, sacks of chickpeas, sweets, and sultanas brought by boat from Karachi. It was a badger sett: close, mephitic and possessing the threat of danger, Netherlandish brushstrokes painting the faces with depths and shadows.

The ardent young Saudi who had stood over him on the beach and fired his gun into the air and covered him in his headscarf breathed in close and fed him sultanas one at a time: Saif was there. Saif the gap-toothed, who was also known as Haidar, the lion, because he was a suicide bomber who had done all that was asked of him: whose vest had not exploded, and so was between the living and the dead, invincible, a martyr who went among them still.

Saif's smile was misleading; he was calibrated, in this other respect a detonation waiting to happen, prone to violent mood swings and other reversals. He had memorised scenes from *Pink Panther* films, poured sweet tea for the poor, slit the throat of a student in Jeddah, and without regret threw a grenade into a video shack in Mogadishu, killing those inside for the crime of watching a Bollywood film.

Yusuf picked up mobiles at random and texted orders to the battle lines. When he finished he scooped rice into his mouth with his fingers and sipped tea. He ate in silence. He stood up and stepped over the legs of his men with care and courtesy. He paused over James, read aloud the words on the Englishman's T-shirt, and continued out into the starry night.

A wind blew in off the sea. The courtyard of the mosque was sifted with sand. Yusuf washed his hands and feet and entered the mosque. He carried a lamp into the dark and knelt behind a pillar in the back and prayed. The jihad had been hard. His men had fought Ethiopian soldiers, African Union peacekeepers from Uganda and Burundi, and the Somali Transitional Government troops and its allied militias. At one time in Mogadishu the Ethiopians fired in phosphorous shells with a petroleum-jelly-like napalm which ignited and burned through shacks and stuck to the flesh of his men and smouldered through them. There was another offensive where they had to scrape together the pieces of the boys who had been directly hit by mortars and gather them for a funeral. He had resorted to the methods of Iraq, hiding among the poor, using them as decoys, placing improvised explosives in the marketplaces, and training suicide brigades for attacks on Crusader targets.

On the day they made love for the first time, she spoke to him about her work. They were sitting by the table in her room. Her papers and photocopies were stacked at one end. The filing cards were loosely arranged at the other. In the centre of the table was a glass ashtray. She pulled from among her papers an aerial photograph of a ship. It was her way of easing into the subject.

'The research vessel *Knorr*. Home port: Woods Hole, Massachusetts. It carries all of the instruments that are meant to assist oceanographers. On longer expeditions there is often a submersible on board.'

It was summertime on the Arctic Ocean. There were fragments of ice. The decks were arranged in rectangles. There was a hangar at the back of the vessel. It struck him as industrial compared to the whaling ships in the paintings hung in his family home, which were curved, studded with whale teeth along the rails. Then again, what he did know? He was a paratrooper who had become a spy.

'I have a French view of science,' she said. 'Very romantic. Don't get me wrong. I am sensible. It's just I have to stop myself from falling for comments like "exploration is a hunt whose prey is discovery".' She lit another cigarette. 'Anyway, I've never worked in France. When I began my doctorate I divided my time between Zurich and a town called La Spezia in Italy. Do you know it?'

'No.'

'The locals call it Spesa. It was convenient; not so far along the coast from my parents' place. It's the Italian naval base for the Ligurian Sea. There's a lovely mural by the Futurist Prampolini in the town post office. There's also a submerged statue of Christ in the harbour, a few metres down. You can't see it, but I always felt it under me when we headed out, the hands stretched up' – she held her two hands over her head – 'blessing all the boats passing above.

'The Ligurian Sea is one of the deepest parts of the Mediterranean. It looks like this' – she doodled with a pencil a gash on a line she indicated to be the sea floor – 'it goes down to 2850 metres. An underworld within touching distance of the Riviera. Amazing.

'I'd gone to Spesa to work on a NATO project to protect the Cuvier's beaked whales in the Ligurian Sea. They needed a

52

mathematician to understand how noise reverberated in the undersea canyons. The hope was to track the diving range of the Cuvier's and see if the navy sonar was damaging them. There were dolphins in the Tigulian Gulf and fin whales, pilot whales and very occasionally sperm whales further out. In my work I only had eyes for the Cuvier's. They're rough-toothed whales.' She sketched one. She was a teacher. 'Seven metres long from short beak down its sloping head to its tail fin, here. They're shy and difficult to spot. They live to eighty.'

Her drawing made them look like dolphins.

'Are they playful?'

She thought about it. 'No, I wouldn't say so. They're hard to place. At first I felt they hadn't grown up, that they were childlike, but the more we studied them, the graver their lives seemed to be. What is really interesting about them is how deep they go. They are the deepest diving creatures in the world. They stay underwater for an hour, to a depth of 2000 metres, using sonar to hunt for squid there.'

'Drink?'

'Not for me.'

He poured himself a whisky.

'I appreciated the way they looked, they were pretty things, chalked up under the jawbone, with heavily lidded eyes. The work wasn't challenging, I grew tired of it, by the end the whales did not interest me any more than a partridge, or one of those funny three-legged dogs you sometimes see in the parks in London. The Cuvier's are K-selected under the constant conditions of the ocean: slow maturation without predators; large brains, long gestation and low birth rate. If I had been an engineer like you I suppose I might have been interested in how they were at one time rendered for watch oil, causing the seconds to tick on Swiss watches.' She tapped her dial. 'If I was a biologist I would definitely have been interested in how they can't swim into the rivers that flow into the Ligurian Sea because their kidneys can't clean out the bacteria that's in freshwater. I probably should have marvelled at their intelligence. Instead there I was on the boat, and the boat was tipping, the boat is always tipping, listening

53

for them, first at this many fathoms, then deeper, and . . . do you know what a whale sounds like underwater?'

'A cow?'

'Like a piece of plastic bending and snapping. Or sometimes tele-phonic clicking. Finally I got the message. The Cuvier's were showing me the way, that was all. Nothing was the same after that. Instead of looking at creatures, I started looking at the sea itself, how it filled the canyons, and what is it like at the bottom, what happens there.

'I think I first started to think of this when my colleagues began to study the decompression the Cuvier's suffered when they came up for air, they came up and it was as if they had left the world and the coming back to it was violent. They stay motionless at the surface and we still don't know whether it is the pain of the bends, the osteonecrosis fizzing in their bones, or that they are blinded by the light.

The strategy of the jihadists allied to al-Qaeda in Somalia is to create chaos in order to establish a supreme Islamic nation pure in its religion: a caliphate of Greater Somalia at the forefront of the global jihad. Local and foreign fighters will strike at Christian Ethiopia and Kenya, seeking to liberate the Muslims in those countries, thereby dragging America, Europe and the other Crusaders into the fray. The goal of the global jihad is to replicate itself through force of arms, creating a Muslim superstate: intercontinental, without borders, adjudged by the same laws and united by prayer.

Yusuf prostrated himself behind the pillar in the mosque by the sea. He was a zealot, a soldier, an Arsenal football club fan, and Allah alone knew he prayed for clearness of mind and motive. He prayed for religious men. He prayed for the submission of Somaliland and the return of the Ogaden to Somalia. He prayed for the city of Mogadishu. He prayed that the thieving and whoring pirates be dragged by their hair into the burning presence of God, or else be strangled.

He was al-Afghani – the Afghan – because he had trained at the al-Qaeda camps in Afghanistan as a sniper, then in tactics. He had been a bodyguard to Abdullah Azzam in Peshawar until Azzam's assassination. He had later been assigned to protect Hamza bin Laden, one of Osama's younger sons. It was Azzam who laid out the path for Yusuf to follow: jihad and the bullet alone; no negotiation, no dialogue, no surrender.

He had been with Osama bin Laden in Tora Bora in 2001 for some days. He returned home to Somalia in 2002 a few weeks after escaping a raid on a safe house in the Asir mountains in south-western Saudi Arabia. When the counter-terrorism police burst in they found a bowl of porridge steaming on the table and a stack of passports from different African countries, each with Yusuf's photo on them, each with a different name. The escape was celebrated on jihadist websites and bundled on videos along with bomb attacks and decapitation of infidels. Yet it was only a deception: an inside man in the Saudi police redirected the search team while Yusuf scrambled down a cliff.

He was at war with the warlords and the faithless others who had destroyed Somalia after the collapse of the Siad Barre regime in 1991. They were illiterate, syphilitic, irrational killers. But then, so were his men. The jihad attracted more than its share of sociopaths. What he needed were boys with pure motives who were prepared to go into battle, or strap explosives on and blow themselves up. He had spent his childhood as a shepherd in Somalia and he knew how tough and resourceful and undismayed boys were and always preferred them to men, who were unreliable, or who were in the jihad for pay or clan loyalty. He personally indoctrinated the boys in his camps: *Kill in the name of Allah! Kill until the end of the world! If you are the last believer, kill! If you are killed, Allah will avenge you. If you are killed, paradise will be yours!* He chanted the Koran. He told the boys how he had found no home in the twentieth century, with its Crusader and Communist empires, with the state of Israel and the Zionist plot, but had found a home for himself in the jihad in the twenty-first century. The boys quieted and hardened the more he talked. They punched the air. They hid their faces in scarves and performed forward rolls down rocky slopes with their machine guns. They were taught to fire mortars by a white-skinned former United States Army Green Beret, who had converted to Islam after serving alongside mujahideen units in the Bosnian war. Yusuf ended the training by talking about the caliphate. *The caliph was coming*, he said, *the holy times were returning.* The caliphate was a state of innocence protected by severe laws, where musicians and all people who acted like strangers were flogged, the hands of thieves lopped off, liars branded, and agitating Sufis, Christians, and Marxists beheaded. There were fewer parties, no cigarettes and no qat.

To pay his way, give to the poor, and support his wives and children, Yusuf traded in frankincense. The money for his militia came in tax revenues and extortion from the towns he governed and private donations from Arab countries. His weapons arrived by dhow from Yemen and the United Arab Emirates, and by plane from Eritrea. He fought alongside the jihadist factions under the command of Muqtar Robow and Hassan Turki, who called themselves the Shabab, or youth; he kept his distance from the rival Hizbul Islam of Hasan Dahir Aweys.

He was sometimes disappointed. Words were used instead of guns, and guns were fired where words would have done. He was a tactician, and his first tactic was absolute trust in Allah, the most merciful, the most benevolent. He had hidden at various times the al-Qaeda operatives wanted for the attacks on the American embassies in Nairobi and Dar es Salaam in 1998 and on Israeli tourists in Mombasa in 2002.

Some of those operatives had been picked off in American air strikes or captured by the Mogadishu warlords and sold on. He himself was always on the move. He spent most of his time in the desert or in the swamps. In towns, he slept in mosques or close to the marketplace. He hid his face, or went in disguise.

He cut out tongues in broad daylight. He won battles. Together, the jihadists controlled south Somalia and most of Mogadishu. He had established terrorist cells of three men in Nairobi and Dubai and he had sleeper agents in Mwanza, Johannesburg, Cardiff and London.

His true beliefs were not much different from the indoctrination he handed out in the camps. He was in it to the death. It was only that he was more experienced. Belief came first for him. For the boys, martyrdom preceded understanding.

Still, there was a question of what religion meant to a jihadist. There was no introspection, except what was needed to look within yourself and decide to die for a cause. There was a detestation of science and an abhorrence of philosophy. Their wives, sisters and daughters were elsewhere. They had not considered a place for them in the caliphate, not even any place they might go and get medical care.

Yusuf prayed and prayed. He looked to the right and to the left. He banged his forehead on the ground. He was leaving Kismayo early in the morning to coordinate the fighting in the Medina district of Mogadishu. The prayer was that he would not be reduced to an animal, like the jihadist commander who smashed in the headstones in Sufi cemeteries for pleasure, and killed an old Italian nun at a hospital in Mogadishu, emptying bullets into her until her body came apart. There was no justice without the possibility of mercy, for instance for the Englishman they had taken hostage.

'Allah, protect me from the fire of hell,' was his last prayer.

'The Cuvier's,' she continued, 'have learned to dive deeper over a million-year evolution. They edged further in from one mutation to the next. Thinking about the way a beaked whale dives is a good way to think about the dimensionality of the ocean.' She selected a softer lead pencil and drew in thick lines on the paper she used for her calculations: a cross section of the planet from its stratosphere to its molten core.

'The oceans cover 70 per cent of the planet surface. You know that. It has five layers. The first is epipelagic. OK. That's wristwatch depth. It contains all the plant life and coral reefs and all the shipwrecks that can be dived with aqualungs; all of Jacques Cousteau. Whatever memory we have of baptism or any other form of submersion is here in blue water.

'The next layer is the mesopelagic. This is the twilight zone, into which blue and all the other colours and light vanish.' She drew more lines. 'Everything under the mesopelagic is night. First the bathypelagic zone, then the abyssopelagic, finally the hadopelagic.'

She looked up. They both did.

'The hadopelagic is what interests me. Hadal from the Greek *hades*, meaning unseen. This,' she said, shading it in, 'is the other world in our world. The only light is the bioluminescence of fish who move under the weight of a thousand atmospheres.'

She drew circles representing the inner parts of the planet.

'There are 3481 kilometres of molten rock and 2690 kilometres of mantle. No one knows much about the mantle. It has no life and therefore no possibility of reanimation and so is without scientific interest. I disagree. I'm studying what I think is the living bit of the mantle, the first few kilometres underlying the Hadal deep. I believe the fissures on the sea floor into the mantle are filled with microbial life.'

Her pencil lingered on the core and mantle.

'The biosphere is the dermis. All life and regeneration in our world belongs to it. Thick as it seems to us, with our histories of evolution and extinction, exploration and colonisation, the abiotic mantle is several hundred times thicker.' She drew another scale showing how nearly all the biosphere was in the ocean.

'We exist only as a film on the water,' she said. 'Of course, this goes against the religion of the Garden of Eden and the canon of political documents ending with the international law of the sea which promote the primacy of man on the planet. Just take a look at it,' she said, running the pencil again over the lines and curves. 'We're nature's brief experiment with self-awareness. Any study of the ocean and what lies beneath it should serve notice of how easily the planet might shrug us off.'

'Wow,' he said.

'We use the words "sea" and "ocean" interchangeably in English, and that's fine, I do it myself, "sea" is a powerful word. A yacht belongs to the sea, it's aimed always to the next port of call. Surfers likewise belong to the sea, not the ocean. You saw how tiny they were on the waves today. How they're spun around like in a washing machine when they fall off their boards. Sometimes they're ground into the bottom. When they ride out a wave, it carries them home, to land. The sea has its transformative power, its own history. I told you my mother is from Martinique. For Martiniquans the history of the sea is slavery. The sea goes across, that's the point. The sea is a pause between one land-bound adventure and another. It joins lands. The ocean goes down and joins worlds.'

She had not even begun with chemosynthetic life and the rest – the refractory molecules of anoxgenic photoheterophotic bacteria – but she could not recall having spoken so acutely with a lover. Perhaps it was because they were so close to the Atlantic, or that he lived in Africa and she would not see him again, or perhaps it was the opposite, that she would see him all the time.

They talked into the night and were awake to each other. The upright-ness of the chairs worked against intimacy. There had already been a consummation and their courtship was subsequent; in talk, not in the silence of touching.

He felt a brittleness inside him. He was not able to share his career with her, and it was the imbalance in their conversation that perhaps made him speak about the Midgard serpent, which lived so enormously in the ocean the Norsemen believed it encircled the world.

'Do you know the story?'

'Vaguely,' she said, 'hardly.'

'The bond which held the Midgard serpent in was the weight of the sea itself, which was too heavy to push away. The serpent had a sister and a brother. The sister, Hel, became Death. She was given power by Thor to send the dead into nine separate worlds. Her table was made of hunger, the walls of her house were built with agony, and the mortar was horror. The serpent's brother was the wolf Fenrir. He was bound by chains made of the opening and clamping of fish gills, the footfall of a lynx, the roots of stones under a glacier, the moods of bears and the droplets on the talons of an eagle dropping down on a lamb.

'Of these three siblings it was the Midgard serpent who remained alive in longest in the sea.' He smiled. 'I mean the ocean.'

'Who was the father?' she asked.

'Loki, the god of mischief. Of course, he ended up badly too. Odin had him chained to a rock and venom spat into his face.

'His writhing caused earthquakes underwater.'

She got up and stretched herself.

'The Greeks,' she said, touching her toes, 'believed in Okeanos, the ocean about the equator shown on the shield of Achilles which kept the known world afloat.'

She told him this and they spoke about Atlantis. She said nothing of Sumer and Enki; Abzu was as private to her as numbers were.

She instead spiralled down the axis of time in the ocean. She held up for him the example of the orange roughy.

'It is a fish that takes forty years to reach maturity and lives to one

hundred years on the seamounts, but it has been fished nearly to extinction in a generation.

'Let's say the Atlantic is 160 million years old,' she continued. 'It
might be older. We appeared less than one million years ago. We walked
in yesterday. It's not much of a claim. Yet somewhere in the Atlantic
right now and in the other oceans, some man, I'm sorry, it's always a
man isn't it, some man is smashing up a seamount more ancient than
any greenwood on land, which he can't see and refuses to value.'

She was taken aback at her own vehemence. She stopped, then began
again. 'Tens of thousands of seamounts have been destroyed in our
lifetime. Any seamount is sure to be demolished the moment it is
located. The chains of those bottom trawlers will break into powder
the cold-water corals and sponges which were there before there was
an English language and which contain in them the most powerful
antibiotics and chemicals which might be used for cancer treatment.
If this was happening in a science-fiction world we would see it clearly
for what it is, but we don't because it's happening here and now. It's
obscured by the money someone is making off it. Scientists are partly
to blame. We're always raising our hands after the destruction has taken
place. There are scientists who become industrial collaborators, bringing
out tailored research for one company or another. I'm lucky to be
working at a depth beyond the reach of industry. They want the
manganese nodules, gold and fuels that are in the deep, but they're too
expensive to get at now. There's still some undisturbed time,' and as
she said this she was thinking very precisely of the abyss, its compass,
duration, its secrets: of species of hagfish older than the Atlantic, who
lived on those sunk from above and tied themselves in knots so as to
give their jaws purchase on the rotting and blanched forms of the dead.

It was already dark. They sat at the desk in silence. It had begun to
snow; again the winter night, again the illuminated sign above the hotel
door spilling out.

These few facts and reflections, which had not even touched on biomathematics, nonetheless set in front of them a common question, which they were too tired to see: is man the joker god Loki, who must be bound in chains?

They had different understandings of time and space. He worked on the surface, the outside of the world. For him, everything was in flux. He was tasking agents to infiltrate mosques in Somalia and along the Swahili coast. He was concerned with alleys, beliefs, incendiary devices; with months, weeks, days, with indelible hours. For her, an age was an instant. She was interested in the base of the corrosive saltwater column, delimiting through mathematics the other living world which has existed in darkness and in continental dimensions for hundreds of millions of years.

'Open your eyes. Open them.'

He did so. It was morning. The smoke-blackened room was empty except for a mujahid – from Chechnya by the look of him – who was squatting by the door breaking apart a Zastava machine gun and placing the pieces in a satchel. The colour coming through the windows and door was blue. Yusuf was dressed like a Mogadishu Bakara market trader in jeans, sandals and a short-sleeved shirt, sunglasses tucked in the pocket. Only the scars of a flesh wound on his neck hinted at his cause and fight.

'You're alive. Good. Drink this,' Yusuf said, and passed him a cup of water.

He drank from it.

The Chechnyan brought over the satchel with the gun in it and, at Yusuf's command, held the oil lamp close to James's face, close enough to feel the heat of the glass. Yusuf moved in behind the lamp. He had shaved off his beard in the night. His face had become massive, scarred.

'Why are you here?' Yusuf asked, in Arabic and the broken English he had learned in Peshawar.

'I've told your men,' he replied, in Arabic. 'I'm a water engineer.' To his own ears, his voice sounded weak and faraway. 'I wanted, I want, to plan a water system for Kismayo. I was invited.'

'Not to do something else?'

'No.'

'We are fighting a war here.'

'I understand, but your people need water.'

Your people. Did Yusuf have any people?

There was the sound of laughter from outside, rare laughter, but it altered nothing in there. There was no equality between them. Yusuf was a Somali, never tiresome about black and white, always superior.

The man's teeth were yellow in the dankness, rodent yellow. The eyes were yellow also, from a liver complaint. Big eyes: he was one of those brigands who never blinked when he pulled a pistol on an unfortunate.

He identified it as a Ceska, a beautiful gun, easy to handle. It must have been a Somali army officer's sidearm from when the country was a client state of the USSR. The grip had been painted over with enamel flowers, most probably in Afghanistan.

'Is your work important to you?'

'Yes, very much,' he said, and like a prayer he said to himself, water be my cover, water cover me.

Yusuf touched the tattoo on his arm with the pistol. A parachute. The regimental badge.

'What is this?' Yusuf asked.

'A mistake. I had it done when I was young.'

'Coming here was a mistake.'

The pistol was jammed deeper into his face. He felt the 0 on his cheek, pressed to his teeth.

'Please, don't. I am needed. Please, please.' He wept. He was shameless. Standing in the sea at the moment he believed was his death he had said nothing, yet now he thought he would say anything to survive, or perhaps he did not believe Yusuf would pull the trigger. The sky was not closing in, he was not turning, no, the pistol was exploratory, another way of getting to know him.

'You have children?'

'No children.'

'A wife?'

'I am not married. My employees rely on me, and so do . . .'

'We will call you Mr Water,' Yusuf said, decisively.

'My name is James. I need to make a phone call to my family. I need to let them know I am alive. We can organise a deal. I am worth more alive than dead. I am worth a sum of money.'

Yusuf held the Ceska by its flowery grip as if to pistol-whip him. 'When we want to know about water, you will tell us. My men wanted to put you to death. I said no, Islam looks gently on the merciful, and your work is merciful. What nation are you?'

'British.'

'Correct. You are British and you are worth nothing. There is no money. The Spanish they pay, the Germans they pay, the British they never pay.'

Yusuf broke into long recitations in Somali. After some time, he made an aside in Arabic. 'How sweet it would be at Eid, if instead of slaughtering an animal in the name of Allah, we would slaughter an unbeliever.'

Involuntarily, James shook. It was a shattered fairytale. Fee-fi-fo-fum! I smell the blood of an Englishman. Be he alive or be he dead, I'll cut off his fucking head. Fictions, none of them buoyant. Yusuf believed that Allah had hung an invisible curtain from the top of the sky to the bottom, separating the believers from the unbelievers. He was looking for quarantine, not Leviathan.

'Do you drink alcohol, Mr Water?'

'Yes, I drink.'

'Alcohol separates you from the Creator.'

'No doubt,' he said. He was rotted through, anyone could see that; his kidneys infected, his piss sea green, and the sun was coming, illu- minating the doorway, the shrine in the courtyard, but he wanted a tumbler of whisky, Macallan, Bell's, Paddy, whatever; some ice, the bottle left open on the floor beside him.

'It is important to me that you are treated generously. It is Allah's wish,' Yusuf said.

'Thank you,' he said, lowering his eyes.

Yusuf demanded submission and James offered it, while the truth of their exchange was that the Somali had ordered him to be held hostage, to be laid in his own waste, and to be beaten there. He had lost a tooth, another two were loose, his nose was broken, his ribs fractured. They had sliced open his hand and shoulder with a blade and in another tussle a mujahid had reached in and grabbed his cock and balls and yanked down on them, tearing a muscle.

It was true. He was worth nothing. Yusuf already had his passport, phone, electronic tablet and other possessions. Her Majesty's Government would never pay for his release. They would not even acknowledge the kidnapping in his case, unless forced to do so by a precise piece of reporting.

Somalia was dried up. The rains had failed. The people were dying of thirst, and he knew better than any real engineer that he was alive only on the promise of water. He was grateful to live on as Mr Water.

'You will go to see the doctor,' Yusuf said, quietly. 'He will take care of you. You will eat, you will drink. Understand?'

He looked away. 'Yes.'

'Hold out your hands,' Yusuf said.

He held them out.

'Take this.' Yusuf placed in his hands a small bottle of perfume with a sticker of a rose on it. 'Open it.'

It was cloying; the substance was sticky, like deodorant dispensed from a plastic ball. 'Thank you.'

Nothing more was said. There was only the tick‑tock of the plastic clock above the door and the sound of the surf and the wind coming through the cracks in the thick walls and the muttering of the mujahid – he was a Chechen. Yusuf stood up and slung the satchel with the machine gun over his shoulder. He sat up and watched the clean‑shaven commander go down the whitewashed steps to the beach and seemingly into the sea.

The Chechen hauled him to his feet.

They were half in and half out of the light and he saw a powder of frankincense on the Chechen's fingertips of a quality that might have been presented to Christ at his Nativity.

The Book of Psalms says the Heavenly Father gathers the waters of the sea together and lays up the deep, as in a treasure house.

What the hell is down there? 91 per cent of the planet's living space, 90 per cent of the living creatures. For every flea, nine sea fleas. No dogs, no cats, but so many other creations with eyes and thoughts, moving in three dimensions. It needs to be explored. With what?

There are only five submersibles in the world capable of diving deeper than 3000 metres. These tiny submarines can spin on a coin, yet have trouble braking in the water column. Among them are the twin *Mir* submersibles of the Russian Academy in St Petersburg; Japan's *Shinkai*, sailing out of Yokosuka; America's *Alvin*, operated by the Woods Hole Oceanographic Institution; and France's *Nautile*, named for Jules Verne's *Nautilus*, jointly operated by the French Navy and IFREMER, the national research organisation. Their operating depth ranges to 6500 metres, or 680 atmospheres, putting 96 per cent of the ocean within reach of man (including most of the Hadal deep), but none of these submersibles are capable of matching the feat of bathyscaphe *Trieste*, which in 1960 touched down on the Challenger Deep of the Mariana Trench; at 11,034 metres, the very bottom of the known world.

An aquanaut is someone who explores the ocean in the same way an astronaut explores space. The first aquanauts were dangled on a cable in a steel ball to depths only those buried at sea had previously plumbed. There were trays of soda lime in the ball to absorb the carbon dioxide the aquanauts breathed out. 'I felt like an atom floating in illimitable space,' one said.

In 1954, two French naval officers made the first dive into the abyss, descending 4023 metres in the waters off Senegal in the FNRS-3 bathyscaphe. This unremarked dive marks the beginning of ocean flight, less celebrated than space flight, but no less heroic.

Because in many ways the ocean is more hostile than space. Space flight is a journey outwards. You can see where you are going, which is why the crews in spaceships generally sit in swivel chairs facing a giant window or screen. Space is about weightlessness and speeds never before achieved by machines and which can scarcely be felt; the discharge of an aerosol is enough to propel a vessel forward, a nudge of a pencil sets its course, and all the while the air inside of it presses against the void outside. Ocean flight is, by contrast, a journey inwards, towards blindness. It is about weight, the stopping of the craft on thermal layers, the pressure of water pushing in, and the discomfiting realisation that most of the planet you call your own is hostile to you. There will never be a Neil Armstrong moment in the ocean. There is nothing to light the way, no prospect, no horizon; even encased in a metal suit the human body is too liquescent to contemplate stepping out onto the deep sea floor.

He was left alone in the courtyard to wash. He was emotional like an animal that had been cornered and then inexplicably left alone. Tears streamed down his cheeks.

Other fighters appeared. They gave him a clean shirt, a clean kikoi and a pair of sandals. They made him wrap his face in a scarf and pull down his shirtsleeves and they walked out together down empty sandy streets and across Kismayo's deserted town square. He looked back over his shoulder and saw the Indian Ocean and something in him was set true at the sight of that expanse, he was straightened out, he was a part of the world again, not a consciousness removed from it, and Kismayo was a beggared town, not part of the madness that had spun too close to the sun. He was out, under the sky, exultant. He walked with sandals on his feet. He was no longer playing memories to himself, he was making them. The fighters flanked him. Their weapons were slung over their shoulders. They wanted to give the impression that he was a white-skinned mujahid, free to come and go as he pleased.

They went by another mosque that was lit with white-and-red neon lights like an ice-cream shop. Next to it was a clinic run by an Iraqi doctor who attended patients in the morning and planned the jihad in the afternoon. Several mujahideen reclined on a balcony on the first floor, eating fruit. On the door to the surgery was a 'No Guns' sticker; a red circle with the machine gun crossed out. It was from an earlier time, when there were aid organisations working in Kismayo. It meant nothing. There were a lot of guns on the balcony and there was a Dushka anti-aircraft gun packed in with sandbags.

He was pushed inside. It was a sterile place, for Somalia. The floor and surfaces were scrubbed. There were buckets of water. The windows and the glass door had been painted on the inside with white paint. There was a medicine cabinet. A woman in a hijab appeared from behind a screen. A nurse. She laid him on an examination bench. She opened his shirt and touched his chest. His head swam. She pressed malaria pills and anti-inflammatories into his hand. The brush of fingertips seemed illicit.

The nurse stood by the door. After a few minutes, a doctor entered and brushed her aside. 'That's my job,' he said brusquely, in English. He addressed James. 'We need blood and urine samples from you.'

Doctor Abdul Aziz. He was not the Abdul Aziz al-Masri, expert in chemical weapons, who served on al-Qaeda's consultative council. He was the man known in Arab intelligence reports as the Iraqi with metal in his arms, who had flown on a Tupolev jet the Sudanese laid on in 1996 to transport the by then impecunious Osama bin Laden from Khartoum to Kabul. He was the doctor who was arrested by Pakistani intelligence in 1999, who had his arms tied to the steering wheel of a lorry and the door slammed on them, shattering them below the elbow. The one who, escaping Pakistan, underwent a number of operations to recover the feeling in his hands, worked as a paediatrician at a polyclinic in Riyadh, learned to hold an infant again, and to write out prescriptions. He was the man who eventually grew tired of life in Riyadh and who travelled to Somalia to give medical care to the poor. He had gone and the jihad had followed, or the other way around.

What was true was when Aziz placed hands, coolly, softly, on his ribs to determine the fractures, it was possible to see the scars on the forearms where the metal pins had gone in, like holes in a ring binder.

Seeing her at work the next morning, he kissed her tenderly on the cheek and went to his room.

He lay on the bed and read the newspapers, then downloaded one of Jacques Cousteau's television shows on his tablet. Even though she had not explained the calculations required for her work, he sensed Cousteau missed the point in the shallows.

If she had attempted to explain her latest paper to him she might have used by way of example the complexity of the maths needed to work with the micromillimetre on the surface of the water which moves between sea and sky and is simultaneously both and something else entirely.

Some of the punch-hole scars on Aziz's forearms were covered by black hairs, others were warmed over in the light cast by the white-washed windows. However, a man cannot be reduced to a single physical detail — a scar, a limp, a squint — except in a police report. His trousers and the crocodile belt that held them up made a more striking impression. They suggested a certain dash.

Aziz's hands were unblemished. James got a good look at them when they rested on his broken nose. The fingers of a pianist: mani-cured, long, thin, alien. it was peculiar how Islamists were set apart by the length of their fingers the way moustaches used to set apart the maniacs of Nazi Germany and the Kremlin and thick necks the lesser apparatchiks.

There was a click and the nose was set with a thumb and forefinger. Aziz took a step back.

'Straight enough.'

'For an infidel,' James said.

Aziz wagged a finger, but his face was friendly, not at all sallow or vulpine.

The doctor indicated his injuries on a wall chart of the human body that had the names of bones written in English and Somali. There was no X-ray machine.

'What about the blood in my urine?'

'Not serious. Drink a lot, Mr Water.'

'My name is James More.'

Aziz gave a hard little laugh. 'More? What kind of name is that?'

'It has its history. What about my groin?'

'That will heal. I will call you Mr Water.'

70

'I have to get out of here. Can you help?'

'No,' said the doctor, smiling.

The nurse floated into the surgery again and stitched the cuts on him under Aziz's direction. Her veil brushed his face. Her breath was scented. She was scented. This time, she was wearing latex gloves. Aziz examined the stitches, nodded approvingly, and the nurse left through the door with the no guns sticker.

'My Somali wife,' Aziz said. 'It is not proper that she approaches you, but this is medicine. We do what we must. Come sit with me.'

Aziz helped him out onto the balcony. It was empty. There was the sound of prayers from the ice-cream mosque and the hammering of a small diesel generator.

'I have been given a box of your belongings. We will have to sell them to pay for your care,' Aziz said. 'Do you agree?'

'I want to return to Nairobi.'

'If Allah permits. Open your mouth. I forgot about your teeth.'

Aziz gave him something resembling a dental pick. With some direction, James picked gravel and tooth chips from his gums and spat the blood and bits into a metal bowl.

He spent the next days on a cot in the surgery. Occasionally he saw the shape of Aziz's wife behind the door, just standing there. He scratched at the white paint in the windows and saw battle wagons parked in the street and a guard sitting in the shade of a mango tree with a Kalashnikov that was inlaid with beryl and glittered.

One evening Aziz brought a plate of bread and pieces of goat meat and they shared a meal.

'I'm sorry for what's happened to you, Mr Water,' Aziz said. 'So many of the mujahideen are uneducated. There should be a ban on taking in boys who cannot read. They need to study the Koran themselves in order to decide on their sacrifice. There should also be a ban on injecting the suicide bombers with drugs meant to limit their ability to think.'

'They do that?'

'I once saw it in Mogadishu. I was very ashamed. I am told they do it in Pakistan. But Pakistan . . . It is not a good practice.'

'Why are you talking to me?'

'You will be gone soon, one way or another.'

'What do you mean by that?'

Aziz squeezed his hand. 'They will not kill you. Yusuf made a promise.'

They were the kindest words that had been spoken to him in his captivity. 'Thank you.'

'There is no one to talk to here with an education. Besides,' Aziz's voice dropped to a murmur, 'you cannot trust Somalis. You give them money to buy medicine for the clinic and they send it to their family. You give them phone credit and they use it to call other relatives. We foreigners do not understand how attached Somalis are to themselves. The true religion of a Somali is Somalia. I tell you they are weak in all the practical parts of the jihad. There was a boy among those who sleep here who would without hesitation have given his life for the jihad. The other day his uncle came to visit. Whatever he said was worse than death or hell to the boy; in a minute he set down his gun and walked away, refusing to say a word to anyone.'

James nodded. Somalia was irregular. Hardly any foreigners visited it, yet there were Somalis all over the world. There was internet in one neighbourhood, in the next the people were dying of thirst. You could receive money through a wire transfer, but you could not keep your child alive.

On another evening, Aziz asked about water.

'What do you suggest we do about the wells in Kismayo?'

'That is what I came here to find out.'

'The water is too expensive for the poor.'

He had prepared for this moment in Nairobi and in the dark before becoming Mr Water.

'Does the local authority have control over all of the water sources?'

'What do you mean?'

'You need to drive out the water profiteers by any means necessary. Once all the wells are under the administration they need to be marked on a map and the details of each put in a public record.'

Aziz pulled out a notepad and a biro and made notes in Arabic. It was difficult for him. He held the biro like a stirring spoon.

'You need to know the depth of each well and the quality of the water in it. The closer the well is to the sea, the more likely it is to be brackish. In the slums, it might be contaminated with sewage. You need to know how many people are using it. You plot all of this on the map. Then you can start to think about setting a fair price for each well.'

'What if the people still cannot afford to pay?'

'They should get the water at no cost. You will need a ration card system. In return for clean water, families will build drains and rain-water tanks. The local authority will have to monitor the water supply and educate the women in water conservation. Eventually, it will need to drill boreholes, secure the spring water and build a sewage treatment plant. I can help you with all of this.'

'You already are,' Aziz said, and took his hand.

Aziz had had three wives. The first was Iraqi; she had died. The second worked as a doctor in Riyadh. The third was the Somali. His Iraqi wife had belonged to a Muslim sect that retained pagan elements of star worship. She was fifteen when they married, eighteen when she died giving birth. There was no question Aziz was sincere in the antenatal and postnatal care he provided in the Bari slum, which spilled out onto one of the beaches. It had tripled in size since the Islamists had taken control of Kismayo.

'In such a place,' Aziz said, 'only the air is free. There is no comparison between life there and life in Riyadh. Hardly a day goes by without a baby in my care dying of some curable sickness. The people have no work. They have not enough food. They have no school and this is something we want to correct. Three families share a shack,' he went on, 'there is terror of fire, especially on hot days. A spark flies on the wind and lights the palm thatch and paper. People are burned alive. It is worse when it rains. Then the mud mixes in with the waste from the latrines. I do believe,' his voice rose, 'with so many people packed in such conditions, Somalia will generate a plague that could spread across the world.'

'Cholera?'

'A new plague.'

'You could make a weapon of it,' he said.

Aziz reached over and slapped him in the face, just one slap. 'I am a doctor.'

His face flushed with anger. 'You keep company with killers.'

It was true. Aziz had clinical knowledge and served others, yet he also had a weakness for sermons he could not quite hear, for battle banners, for scimitars flashing far away. His venture was for the jihad, not for humanitarian action. He missed his family, he loved them, it was not easy to live with the secret of being a mujahid. He was choleric. He had fits of rage and the division within him intensified the hatred. Many sentences would begin, I cannot allow the pigs to . . .

They were quiet, then Aziz said, 'There is cholera here already.'

'You should report it.'

'Here? To whom would I report it?'

'To the United Nations.'

'Never.'

'You need help.'

Aziz's eyes narrowed. 'The Crusades have not ended.'

'What?' He said what, but he knew what was coming.

'The United Nations is a cover for the Crusaders. The United Nations is the Knights of the Cross.'

'Even UNICEF?'

'Especially UNICEF!'

He regarded the punch-holes on the doctor's arm, the belt buckle.

'Such an organisation! Which claims so much for itself but delivers so little to the children? Would you like to know what I really think?'

'Yes.'

'I think the Crusaders are led by the Jews!'

If these words were written down they would look deranged, but Aziz spoke them with feeling; he had some notion the jihad was a cure and the fighting was the cutting out of a tumour under improper conditions.

'What is necessary,' Aziz said, more calmly, 'is to turn the Crusaders and their slaves back from the Muslim land of Somalia, so the people can live in a true Islamic state.'

He was exhausted. He had to respond. He spoke with care, the words came out like stones and pebbles. 'Is it more important to get help for the women and children you see in your clinic, or to follow the jihad?'

'I see it as one treatment. Medicine is a mercy, the jihad is a duty.'

'What about me? Am I a Crusader? I came here to bring water.'

'You are a part of it,' Aziz said, unhesitatingly. 'Allah will ask payment of you.'

'You said I was going to be spared.'

'La, la, la. How can I know the will of Allah. You may die. You may become a blessed one.'

The Ligurians were split in the Punic wars between Carthage and Rome and remain divided today. There are the muggy streets of Spesa on the coast of Liguria, with rubbish, fish heads rotting on the dock in the sun; and there is the rain and bracing air of the surrounding Ligurian Alps, with vineyards, olive groves, apricots, figs and nuts on the lower slopes, cheese production and game higher up, and ducks netted on the icy tarns in the migratory season.

Her cabin was high on a mountain overlooking the Ligurian Sea. It had a slate roof. The walls were of stones, logs and moss gathered from the slopes. The windows were square; four panes each. There were always flowers in the window boxes when she was there. Her flat in South Kensington was of the sort Peter Pan might visit, whereas the whole effect of the cabin – the doors and mantles carved with faces and with shapes of animals, the light slanting in, the air, the shreds of cloud and sea through mist and sleet, through trees – was of a scene a wooden puppet might have woken up to in his most resinous childhood.

The mountain was Janus-faced. One side was sunlit, with slopes of Aleppo and maritime pine. The other was dark. Snow lingered for months; there were Alpine meadows, oaks and chestnuts, and bogs into which deer sank up to their nostrils. It drizzled more often on that side. The farmhouse where she bought her supplies was obscured and could be seen only by the smoke curling up from its chimney. Heading upwards with a pack pony, she was often bathed in sunshine the moment they turned from the landward to the seaward side. On such days she would strip off her hunting jacket and continue up the stony path sweating under the sun, her steps slow with her heavy pack. They raised red partridge from the undergrowth, the dust quivered, and their footsteps resonated off the oldest exposed rocks on earth. It was not the reason she bought the cabin, but it had become an attraction: her property had never been sunk in the Ligurian Sea, or any other. If she were immortal, she could sit on the mountain under the moon and stars – the snow globe – and not get her feet wet in a million years.

He waded out into the river and for a few steps was covered by the waters.

He used to go to the Saracen's Head in Church Street with his sister and her friends and never considered the picture on the pub sign until he had joined the secret intelligence service. He was raised to think of the desert as a desolation, as an absence. The Christian prayer he was given as a child to recite at bedtime, the smell of soap, the towels, brass doorknobs, the heaviness of home, with the rain sweeping in off the North Sea against the window, held the milk and honey of heaven to be beyond the desert.

Aziz's childhood was his own turned inside out. His family owned an oasis under a cliff near the Syrian border. They drove there from Baghdad in the season in a dazzling convoy of cars. The cliff blocked out the sun. It was wet with dew at dawn. Water was plentiful. Workers grew vegetables in a field. Metal taps gushed into cement troughs. Camels drank their fill. The horses had their own drinking place. The tents were pitched out of the wind, away from the animals. When Aziz was a small child and it was cold at night, he was sometimes made to sleep outside, covered with sand to keep warm.

He was the Arab who grew up in a binary world, which went zero one zero one one desert city desert city city. In Baghdad, he drank a can of Coke before reaching the till. He watched Westerns. His best friend had computer games. A boy from his football team spoke of sexual encounters with a maid. There was the dictatorship, the war with Iran, the fume of cars on the motorways in the city, the way the overpass curled up and across. In the desert, there were only the horses and the medical studies he continued in the tent, brushing sand away from the textbooks every few minutes. Nothing was made there except leather. Every living thing in the desert seemed to him to be precious, to have a fixed number and to exist in such a way as to make him feel like a created being. It was no place. It extended through Iraq into Saudi Arabia and all the way to Oman. He took his horses and rode out across it; a sea at the centre of the world, with unfathomable sands, shifting and undulating. Aziz had this in

77

common with James: if he had no sense of duty, he would have returned to his horses.

The prayers in the desert were different, inexpressibly cooler to accommodate the heat. Aziz's understanding of the greatness of the Koran came on those nights when the constellations shone in such depth and number that only Allah could accommodate them and every ideology looked insignificant set against them.

Danny's colleagues were atheist or agnostic, except for the Anglican, who was struck by a car one afternoon on the Fulham Road. This colleague fell into a coma and her family asked for prayers to be read at her bedside. Danny was reluctant, but it was not a moment to stand on principle. She turned up at the hospital and was given the canticle 'Benedicite Omni Opera' to read.[1] The words disturbed her. Before any mention of the earth or the sun was a line surely lifted from Sumer:

O ye Waters that be above the Firmament, bless ye the Lord: praise him, and magnify him forever.

Her colleague went on to make a full recovery. She herself could not let go of the waters behind the stars. She calculated that if such a sea were only the depth of our solar system and the same terms applied, the pressure of atmospheres in its Hadal deep would be so great that the fish there would have no skeletal structure and would move like apparitions.

---

[1] *Benedicite, aquae omnes, quae caelos sunt, Domino, benedicat omnis Virtutis Domino.*

James developed a sense of ease with Aziz. The Iraqi protected him from the more unbalanced among the mujahideen. They talked about America.

'You talk about achievement. What is the achievement of a shopping centre?'

'This is student stuff,' he said. 'Why always shopping? America put a man on the moon.'

'So they claim.'

'Look to yourself. Saudi Arabia is ready for a revolution. All the people do is shop. There is nothing else for them. The country is in a social coma.'

'The majesties feed in this way it is true,' Aziz said uncomfortably, then changed the subject.

Aziz had no idea about government and had not studied politics, philosophy, history or economics. He was like a common or garden Evangelical, who reckoned by faith alone his clinic would be raised into a health service. Thomas More would have picked apart Aziz's worldview in a moment. Not because it was a vanity of a Musulman, but because it was dystopian. The caliphate was as uninspired as it was unmerciful, with no basis in common law.

He accepted there was something ill in Western civilisation; an apple-sized swelling in the armpit. Any clear-minded person could feel it. It was true also that he had with his own eyes seen simplicity and compas-sion in the Muslim world, how the sick and old were cared for within the community. But that was as far as he went.

They had both killed. James had done it in under orders in the military. Did that absolve him? Aziz had killed on account of personal convic-tion, the emotion carried him, the affront. He perhaps heard the sentence

79

al-Qaeda wanted carried out: *Death to the enemies of Islam by the bullet, by bombs, alcohol, narcotics, rumour, assassination, strangulation, chemicals and other poisons*. Aziz was conflicted. A part of him looked with sympathy on James and believed he could become a Muslim. Another part believed there was a space in the Englishman's chest where his heart should have been – that he was not born whole.

They lied to each other. Aziz had not come to Somalia of his own accord. In the messages he sent to Saudi Arabia he complained of a lack of money and planning and a difficulty in communicating with al-Qaeda leaders in Pakistan. Somalia did not have the advantage of Afghanistan, which sheltered fighters and supplied opium to the world. Some of the messages were also filled with nostalgia:

> How I wish our enchanted evenings in Afghanistan would return! That dream has passed and produced bitter fruit, but some is the fruit of paradise!

There will be no more open battles in Somalia. The jihadists learned that lesson when they overreached themselves in 2006. They had stood on the border with Ethiopia and declared a holy war on Ethiopia, and for that they were annihilated. The Ethiopians invaded Somalia in a matter of days. They took Mogadishu without a fight and chased the jihadists south to Kismayo. There was a brief battle there in which the jihadists were routed. Hundreds of them retreated to the mangrove swamps along the Kenyan border. These are impenetrable places, with tropical bays, shallows and tidal channels, septic, simmering, with flora and fauna of every scent and hue. Some days passed and then the American AC-130 gunship flew in from Djibouti. The Ethiopian MiGs had already flown sorties from Debre Zeyit and cut up a convoy of jihadist lorries stuck in the mud. But the Ethiopians had nothing to match the Tartarean armaments of the Americans. Without warning, from 20 kilometres away, the gunship filled the mangrove with shells the size of Coke bottles and shredded and vapourised and blew the holy warriors out of this life. It took a moment for the shells to fill the air across the target area the size of a football pitch. There were few survivors. Some escaped inland up the dry riverbeds – the wadis – others went on foot or by dhow into Kenya.

Predictably, these same fighters returned to Somalia and built a new and more radical organisation, with a heightened martyrdom complex, recapturing south Somalia town by town. They discredit merchants who oppose them and dismantle their businesses. They tax goods and livestock coming and going: fuel, rice, pasta, the narcotic leaf qat, which Somali men chew to get high, and all the market stalls down to the fish on their slabs.

The lesson of 2006 has been taken to heart. A jihadist must know how to hide on the land and in the swamps. Somalia is wild. It is from another time. It is possible to live in the scrub with a gun. A man can recite his prayers far from any road, experiencing a sense of holiness, hardening himself. It is not a secure refuge – its fruits are bitter-tasting as Afghanistan's once were – but it holds a similar promise of paradise. That is why Somalia serves as a trapdoor for Saudi Arabia. Young Saudis are sent there to lay low and to learn how to fight. They are marginal characters – on the run from themselves as well as from the police – withdrawn, stammering, younger brothers, with unresolved inner conflicts, most of them sexual.

She abandoned the beaked whales, left Spesa behind, but kept the cabin in the mountains. She completed her doctorate in Zurich, and remained in the morbid heights of Switzerland for seven years. Her interest in the deep became sharper. It also became more poetic, fed by visits to the Sumerian archive at the University of Zurich.

In those years she liked to board a train to the Alps with her bicycle, choosing the platforms at Zurich main station at random. She found there was veracity in the claim that, in landlocked countries, espionage takes the place of adventure, and police take the place of pirates. Nevertheless, she pushed on into the deepest valleys, the ones which lost their winter sun in the early afternoon. She biked along the valley floors and visualised the day they would be at the bottom of a new sea. The steepness of the slopes matched those of the Mid-Atlantic Ridge. Waterfalls plunged off rock. They fell in the air, through air. She prefigured them as underwater cascades, water pouring through water. She pictured the ski pistes on a sonar display, the chalets lit up by pinpricks of light, the heated municipal swimming pools as hydro-thermal vents thick with mats and carpets of microbial life and not day-trippers from St Gallen.

'I go to Switzerland once a year,' he said to her, in bed in the Hotel Atlantic.

They shared memories of Zurich airport. If by some new method these images were downloaded from their minds they would correspond. They had similar sensibilities, and a similar way of watching the flow of people and landscapes and framing them. They had both looked out of the windows of the air terminal to the cow pastures and forest, the streams flowing to Lake Zurich, the inferior coffee in a white china *demitasse*, the snow on the Alps, while around them was a constant motion of humans and machines, families walking to their gates, the airport train gliding in, the Swiss planes circling above, white crosses on red, but these images were differently settled in their minds.

She retained hers as something familiar; the landscape she looked out upon as a student, the system she worked in. He arrived in Zurich from poorer countries and was uplifted. He saw through the window a display of labour and efficiency which stood in contrast to the Muslim communities he was charged with observing.

They came to the edge of the wood. They wanted to reach the village.

'I'm sorry,' she said quickly. 'I can't go in.'

He already had a foot in the wood. He turned. She was teetering. 'Are you all right?'

She looked into the wood. The branches and ferns made her nauseous.

'I'm fine,' she said. 'No, I'm not. Oh, I think I'm going to be sick.'

The trees sliced away the day, producing narrows and shadows on the snow and polygons whose angles were irresolvable.

'Come away,' he said, and he put his arm around her and walked her out into the field, into the light. He made her drop her head and breathe deeply. Her recovery was instantaneous.

'I don't understand,' she said. 'I've no history of claustrophobia. Not even in a submersible.'

They set off in another direction.

'When I was a boy,' he said, as they walked in open space, 'we had horses that refused to jump. They had cleared hedgerows and ditches without question, then suddenly were afraid of heights.'

'I'm a horse?' she said with mock displeasure.

'I'm saying you might be afraid of the dark.'

Kismayo is famous for its magicians and for the refreshing breeze blowing in off the Indian Ocean at night. The great Muslim travellers visited the town, so did Zheng He and his Chinese fleet. The Portuguese

83

built a fort there, which the Omanis captured. The Somalis drove out the Omanis, then yielded to the Italians.

The town broke down during the civil war and continues to deteriorate. Its population is growing rapidly as a result of the large numbers of internally displaced. Half of its people are under eighteen years old. There are few schools. There are hardly any jobs.

The port no longer has any warehouses. The Taiwanese tuna boats are gone, chased away by the pirates. But the dhows still bring in diesel, cement and crates of bullets, and they still take away fish, bananas, mangoes, coconut matting, and animals, always animals. It is a scene at night. Black waters lap within, lanterns and fires burn on the quay. It is loud, heaving with livestock. The beasts are walked down to the port at dusk from their grazing at the edge of the town. The camels are roped together three at a time and hoisted onto the vessels. It is remarkable to see how the handlers whisper religious verses into their ears to calm them before they are lifted.

They allowed him to walk with them in town one evening to witness a feeding that had been set up for the people sleeping rough in the port. Several men went with him. He was ordered to conceal his face. He felt stronger. He saw things more clearly. It was beautiful to go forwards as if through walls. They went by shattered buildings and others not completed. He looked at one structure and knew from its exterior that it was where he had been held.

A crowd of boys played a game of table football on a street corner. They dropped their hands to their sides and fell silent as the fighters went by. There were candlelit stalls of women who told fortunes, and women who painted henna patterns onto hands and wrists. There was a hair salon called Le Chinoise lit with a single electric bulb. A woman in a veil pushed by him in a narrow street. Her eyes flashed. They turned a corner and there was the overpowering smell of the fish market and the trilling voices of women selling the last of the day's catch. Girls scavenged through a rubbish heap. Older women sat on a wall further on, not veiled, still wearing their daytime facemasks: red from avocado to protect against pimples, yellow from sandalwood to protect from the sun. There were so many women out in the world. In his captivity there had only been Aziz's Somali wife, who placed her hands on his broken chest. In one dark alley they told him to kneel and look away while they urinated against a coral wall. There was a stale smell of piss. The alley was a urinal. A cloud of mosquitoes rose up.

They walked by the shore. Fruit bats fell from the palm trees and flew out and touched the sea and other fruit bats circled a minaret, as big and indecent as dogs. It was the same minaret Kismayo's last Catholic stole up with his trumpet, to protest against the intolerance of the Islamist regime. He was an old man, cogent, certain of himself, who had played in the town band during the Italian period. The band wore a green uniform with gold epaulettes and had a repertoire of military marching songs of the Italian Alpini regiment, anthems, polkas from the Tyrol, and dance numbers of the day. But when the Catholic took his trumpet up the minaret he had a mind to play a piece of jazz. Alas, there was no time. They were already after him, charging up the narrow staircase, so, instead, impulsively, he seized the loudspeaker and spoke 'Hail Marys' for all that part of the town to hear, the words clanged on the ears of the believers, until there was a grunt, which was the old man being knocked over the head with a brick. They dragged him down the steps. He was almost beaten to death. To save his life, his family declared him mad and dispatched him to Kenya.

They kept a gun trained on him. They did not speak English or Arabic. It was disconcerting. Their faces were covered and it was not possible for him to interpret their body language. They walked across the beach to the port and that troubled him too. He was a strong man, but the mock execution had traumatised him. He took off his sandals and felt the warm sand between his toes. The fighters would have walked barefoot even in the middle of the day. They had no nerves left in their feet. The wind blew and raised the sand in places into eddies. At the water's edge there were eels writhing and feeding on washed-up tuna and crabs of many sizes and patterns of shell scuttling sideways back to their holes.

The port was packed. Two dhows were tied up. Dirty goats were being thrown onto them. They bleated in the air and landed on the deck; square on their hooves. They were headed for Mecca, to be slaughtered there by pilgrims.

The famished were all around, pressed in with the animals; weaker than them, more dazed. They had staggered in from the dead country. There was nowhere else for them to go. Some slept under the lorries, or along the coral wall. Their mouths were full of dust. They were hollow-cheeked; in some faces the narrowness produced a rodent-like expression. Several hundred of them were in the overgrown garden of an abandoned villa, waiting to be fed a meal. Other fighters were already there, cudgelling them into a line. The food was cooking in a cauldron on an open fire. A stray dog stepped forward and shat in the dust, then moved back into the bushes. Some people fainted before they reached the food and there was no one to lift them up. The fruit bats went by, brushing low. They had fur bellies and beads for eyes. Their teeth were sharp, overlapped and interlocked.

There was some delay. He could not see what. A rock was thrown. Possessions were thrown up in the air. A baby was trampled, then recovered. The man who threw the rock was pointed out and executed with a shot through the mouth and then there was just the sound of the food being served and the scraping of hands against the bowls.

The bare wooden floor of the billiards room was scattered with sawdust. A stove threw out thick waves of heat, like in the railway station waiting room in La Roche. The unvarnished card tables were inset with leather. Low hanging lights illuminated the billiards tables. He rolled balls across the felt. The japanned reds and whites clicked and the completeness of their colours resembled the sound of their clicking.

The room smelled like a city villa and a sanatorium; Swiss. On little plinths around the room were marble busts of historical figures. He went over to where she was sitting, under Garibaldi's head. They were cold from their walk and were turned towards the stove. Pastries and hot chocolate were brought to the adjoining table. It was afternoon. They played backgammon.

'I've been reading up on the ocean,' he said. 'Is it true that every third breath we take is from oxygen stored in the sea?'

'I wouldn't trust it. It sounds like something a journalist would write. Although' – she rolled the dice – 'it does speak to a larger point.'

'Which is?'

'We're entering an age when everything will be quantified. What we have thought of as abundant we will understand to be limited.'

'The seamounts?'

'I'm talking the world and everything in it.'

'What about fresh air? Will we quantify that?'

'Of course. Oxygen will be a proven reserve. It will have to be managed, just as we manage water and minerals and fuels.'

'The great aqualung in the sky.'

She looked at the board and smiled. 'You're blocked in.'

'I just need a six.'

A three.

'In Rwanda,' he continued, speaking as the water engineer, and as himself, 'they used to have hunting dogs that tracked and killed serval cats in the forests. Princes who lived in grass huts high enough for you or I to stand up in wore the skins. The wicker partition inside the huts spiralled inwards like so' – he danced his fingertips on the card table – 'a snail shell, and the only light came in through a hole in the roof, and the smell was naked; dung, cow blood. You wound in to a grass bed at the centre raised up above the rats and snakes and there was a teenage girl on her knees, waiting for the prince to enter, a different girl from the night before.'

'What's your point?'

'My point is that the prince and the girl belonged to a land of plenty. There was enough then, whereas today every hillside in Rwanda is cultivated. The serval cats and the hunting dogs are gone, so are the grass huts. Nearly all the forest has been cut down, and the perpetrators of the genocide and the victims have nowhere to hide from each other. In some places the wells are running dry, in others the earth is washed away in streams. Rwanda has to develop now, or face another genocide. It's quantified.'

'Very much so,' she said.

He could not get the six he needed to put his final piece back into play. She was overtaking him. They talked on through several more games. Towards the end, she spoke about the future. But when he spoke about dead aid to Africa – how the money given out by charities was wasted – her interest wavered and she became intent on the game.

He tracked tiny movements of small people. Here today, still there tomorrow. He ate sandwiches in the canteen, chaired teleconferences, left the office before rush hour. If he was ever allowed to speak to her about the explosive part of his job, he knew he would not have the words. He would not be able to describe to her the adrenaline rush of lifting and aiming a gun. He would have left her only with a description of the noise a firearm makes when it is fired and the smell of cordite, which lingers.

There was defeatism in their conversation which allowed a greater part to Malthus, he decided, and did not take into account the advances of mankind. Among the busts around the room the only Englishmen were Isaac Newton and John Milton. He looked at Milton – impassive, unseeing – and verse crowded in. The greatest privilege of education, he thought, was to renew and clarify your mind through the perception of others. Milton had more than played his part. Secretary of Foreign Tongues to the Republic; a freethinker who stood to the right of Oliver Cromwell, where the Levellers and Ranters stood to the left: 'Give me the liberty to know, to utter, and to argue freely according to conscience, above all other liberties.'

He thought of how in *Paradise Lost* the Archangel Raphael sat down in Paradise with Adam and Eve, not in the form of mist, but as a hungry creature who needed to eat. He spoke aloud the last lines of Book XII.

'Say it again,' she said. She liked the sound of his voice.

'Some natural tears they dropp'd,' he began, 'but wip'd them soon; The world was all before them, where to choose Their place of rest, and Providence their guide: They hand in hand with wand'ring steps and slow, Through Eden took their solitary way.'

She had suffered from the divide in the English education system, which holds that scientists do not study Milton, and those who love Milton have no comprehension of Newton's gravity, which brought Lucifer tumbling from heaven. But she had recovered to become a voracious reader.

They played billiards. The cues were stacked against a stone sink, where in days past billiard players would have washed their hands and faces. The emptiness of the room and the echo of their footsteps on the wooden floorboards gave the game a slightly eerie feel. Neither of them knew the rules. They made them up. She bent over the table.

'Hell!' she exclaimed. 'I'm terrible. Isn't this longer than a pool stick?'

'Come around this side,' he said.

He moved in behind, wrapped her up, and it began again. She was a flower about to open. He touched her arms and hands. They pulled back the cue, together they struck the white ball, it clicked the red, and for her his kiss was more than the balls striking; he touched her life, she touched his, their lives so independent and far apart from each other.

89

There is a dwarf antelope in east Africa called the dik-dik. They are easier to kill from a distance than to catch. In his intelligence reports he called the fight against jihadists in Somalia the dik-dik war.

But jihadists were more like weeds really, he thought. If you left them alone, they grew thick on the ground. If you cut them down, they came back stronger. So the strategy employed in the dik-dik war was no kind of strategy at all, just a periodic spraying from the air.

A bird flew into the surgery on the same day a girl was stoned to death in the square. It entered with furled wings looking to nest and lost itself, battering itself against the walls and windows. He shouted out when the bird struck him and the guards came in. They wrung the bird's neck and beat him. It lay dead on the floor. Its claws looked like nibs dipped in ink. It was not a songbird. That is also what the cleric declared about the girl who was stoned to death in the town square: 'She's no nightingale.'

They dug a pit and buried her in it up to her neck. The cleric called out that he was doing Allah's instructions. 'I'm not going!' the girl screamed. 'Don't kill me! Don't kill me!'

They gagged her, put sacking over her head and a veil over the sacking, so the world was blacked out. They poured perfume over the sacking. Her waters span impossibly fast, she was retching from within and her hearing must have become more acute, so that imme-diately after prayers were ended she might have heard the men walking across the square – fifty men in all, each of them picking up rocks – and a crowd of hundreds watching, chattering, wailing. She was

90

fourteen years old. She might have heard the men being assembled behind a line drawn in the sand and how each of them dropped their stones at their feet and arranged them in a pile. She might have heard the crowd drawing breath as the men picked up the rocks and at a command hurled them at her head. What a mess they made of it, with their gangly arms, uncoordinated even in the levelling. So many of the rocks missed. And if the girl was never to be saved, if there was no way of going back in time, then the single service that could have been done for her would have been to replace those men with others who could throw and who would choose each stone carefully and throw straight and true, telling themselves the more accurate the throw the more merciful the sentence. That would have ended it. Instead those useless men managed only one strike in the face, smashing the girl's front teeth. They were ordered to pick up their stones and move closer. The crowd surged in anger and there was screaming from the girl's relatives. A young boy sprinted across the square. He was one of her cousins. They had grown up in the same house. He almost got close enough to touch her, but was shot dead just short. The men threw more stones. Some of them hit. Nurses were brought in. The girl was pulled out of the pit. She was examined and found to be still alive, so they slid her back into the hole and packed the sand and gravel around her and the stoning continued. The crowd went quiet. The girl was pulled out once more and declared dead. Her body was laid under the sun, on the world. The nurses shielded her from the men who had stoned her. They wiped the blood and fragments from her face and chest with a wet cloth and washed her for burial. They prayed over her. She was buried under a fig tree in a street near where the boys played table football. Her feet were pointed towards the ocean, her head to the square. She had been sentenced for adultery, after reporting to the religious authorities that she had been gang-raped.

A biblical scene – no, a Koranic scene – the clerics, the men standing behind the piles of stones, the exclamations, the strange trees casting their shapes, the dust itself, the stones flying and missing. It was ancient, also new. The sermon that followed was played over loudspeakers in the town. He had pushed the bird away and listened. Barbed wire was drawn across the square, the gun on one of the Land Cruisers was directed at the crowd. There was a camera recording it for a website. They downloaded the video onto a phone and forced him to watch. No matter how many times it was sped up or slowed down, no matter the cutaway or close-ups, there was no way to correct it: it was an injustice that could never be corrected. If you paused it, he thought, the stones would not stop in the air. If you muted it, the sound would continue.

When the feeding of the people in the port was over, he walked across the town square with the fighters. The moon was out. The square was ashen. The pit was still there. One of the fighters pointed it out. It was filled in with darker earth. A pock.

He fainted one afternoon in the surgery, in the white, and saw Yusuf al-Afghani standing in a wadi in the Somali desert. Clouds passed over. Yusuf's arms were sunk to his elbows in a jar of spermaceti. It shifted, and Yusuf was on the deck of a ship, a sea captain, a brigand, the ship standing still, the sails limp, it was before a tropical storm, all the air sucked out. Then the ship was gone, sunk, and Yusuf stood under a palm tree and he saw the smooth black hands entering into spermaceti. They must be there in the white jar, they could not disappear, but how was it possible to know? What was Yusuf doing? Was he going to anoint himself with a mark of spermaceti oil on his forehead, a blessing at a coronation, or was he going to bring handfuls of the white stuff to his mouth and eat it softly like calf's brain? He watched and was made cognisant of another image, of the Finnish painter Hugo Simberg's wounded angel, carried by two boys, a painting he had seen as a young man in a Helsinki summer long ago, and which forever changed the way he saw the world.

It was a melting in him, visually. There was John More swallowed by a sperm whale off the Patagonian coast and Yusuf with his forearms sunk in a jar of spermaceti, and there was Simberg's angel, and he could not see the connection, except in the whiteness of the windows in the surgery, of the jar, of John More cut by flensers from the whale's belly, the whiteness of the angel's bandage, and the wound beneath; and there was the face of the boy in the Simberg painting, who stared at him as he passed by, a face that could have been his own.

She walked by herself on the beach the next morning. She had left him asleep in her bed – their bed, perhaps – and felt the need to be

J. M. LEDGARD

scoured by the wind, to see the Atlantic, to feel its rhythm, the way the water met and was contained by the land. It was colder than when she had swum and the wind was at her back and seemed to lift her along the shore.

The lighthouse was white with a band of black and a band of orange around the light itself. It was built beyond the breakers on the higher side of a reef. The reef's dingy cracks were infested with insects and molluscs and its plunging walls, rank with glistening seaweed, resembled the palm of a hand outstretched from France, resisting the storms. The door of the lighthouse was high above the reef, approached by slimy steps, and the light was often obscured in the mists. How was it built? First, they raised an iron drum on wooden stilts. Men worked on the lighthouse in fair weather and sheltered in the drum during storms and at night, singing songs and playing the accordion in the dreadful echoing wet. After several years, the windows in the lighthouse were put in and sealed and the workmen rowed back to the shore, leaving a beacon to swing across the bay and out to sea.

She could see the jagged rocks further out to sea on which many ships had foundered. The sailors, fearing being drowned so close to shore, must have called out for an acre of barren ground; broom, furze, anything, in their fear.

The waves were messy, porridgy, falling off before the lighthouse. There were no surfers. She knew how deep it was out there at the horizon. She had these other languages of numbers and sonar. She saw the deepness that was at the edge of France and it made the beach under her feel like a ledge on a cliff.

When she turned around and began walking back towards the Hotel Atlantic the wind almost knocked her over. It was like the skiing in Scotland in her undergraduate days, where the wind came so hard that even dropped into a schuss on the steep slopes she barely moved.

The longest golf drive recorded was hit on the moon. Man has yet to return to the Challenger Deep. The lesson from this is that it is easier for human beings to push outwards than it is for them to explore inwards. The wind that carries you away like a kite will blow you on your back if you turn to face it. Consider how the surface area of a balloon grows when air is blown into it. When we push out, we create new frontiers we might populate. When we take the air out of a balloon, it deflates, and becomes shrivelled.

Millions and millions of years ago we lived in the ocean. When we emerged we had to move in two dimensions, instead of three. That was painful at first. No up, nor any down. We learned to drag ourselves along without legs then with them, going faster and faster, and faster again, by any means. The lack of a third dimension is one explanation for our need to head out over the horizon. Another explanation is that we were raised up from chemosynthetic life in the deep ocean to become photosynthetic life at the top. Having ascended from the eternal night we cannot stop ourselves from heading towards the light. We are moths in the thrall of the sun and the stars, shedding off darkness. That is our instinct, but our conscious nature is also to be drawn to the unknown. We want to know what is behind the wood, what the next valley looks like, and the valley beyond that. We want to know what is in the sky and what is behind the sky. These have been our obsessions since our beginnings, yet the curiosity does not extend to the ocean. We forget there is so much darkness in our world, and to be out on a beach is to be lucky. We know the tides, because they cover the edges of our countries and swell our river mouths and fill our fishing nets, but the connection with the ocean has been lost. If it is described at all, it is as a tomb or a hiding place. Even Tennyson needed the Kraken to batter huge sea worms in its sleep until the last fires heated the deep. *Moby-Dick* is the greatest novel in the English language about the sea.

It is not concerned with the ocean. Only at the end of the book is there a sense of sinking and what is beneath, when the *Pequod* twists into a whirlpool and a death shroud of water closes over it and calms, rolling as it did 5000 years ago. You may have read *Twenty Thousand Leagues Under the Sea*. The distance in the title refers to the journey taken across, not down. If you read it as a child, it would have been an adventure story. As a grown-up, you might be more interested in Captain Nemo's background as an Indian national embittered by the Sepoy mutiny. At any rate, there is nothing of oceanography to be learned from the book. Nemo steers the *Nautilus* down deep, but Jules Verne makes the deep hospitable! There is no weighing of atmospheres, no crushing pressure, no eternal night. When Nemo takes Professor Aronnax on an underwater hike to sunken Atlantis, Verne asks the reader to imagine a forested slope in the Harz mountains in Germany, only underwater.

A nuclear submarine is a killing machine, a destroyer of worlds, yet it is fragile. It implodes when it sinks out of its depth. In 1963, the United States submarine *Thresher* was wrecked with such violence that parts of it were scattered across an area several kilometres wide. There is no comparison between the technology of a submarine going across and the unadorned submersible diving deep. This is because our world is firstly about power and only secondly about knowledge.

Unsurprisingly, most advances in submersible technology have come from secret military projects. The United States Navy developed its own submersibles to clear up its own submarines and to locate and recover fragments of sunken Soviet submarines. A Soviet missile, if recovered, would have been worth years of spying on land. One of these submersibles was called *Deep View*. It had a glass nose and dived into the Sea of Okhotsk. Later there was the *NR-1*. It was powered by a small nuclear reactor and could stay submerged for weeks. The director of the Naval Nuclear Propulsion Programme handpicked its crew of two scientists and ten sailors. It was *NR-1* that recovered a gold sextant from the debris of a Soviet sub, from which the navigator was able to calculate the sub's position, according to the stars.

The Challenger Deep of the Marianas Trench is named after Her Majesty's ship *Challenger*, a Royal Naval vessel whose 1872–75 voyage was the first and greatest oceanographic expedition. *Challenger*'s mission was to plumb the remote seas and trawl them for new life. It was back-breaking and tedious work, but tens of thousands of new species were discovered. Sometimes a hundred creatures never seen before were returned in a single dredge, then nothing for days on end except the commonest fish and whale bones adorned with nodules of metal. Yet we know now that the slime which covered the inside of the dredge each time it was brought up was not the unexceptional ooze the ship's scientist believed it to be. Not whale snot, either. It was all that remained of the most exquisite forms of millions of sea squirts, salp, and jellies, whose diaphanous musculature – more remarkable than any alien species yet conceived – had lost its form in air.

To push inwards is hard, to descend even more so; it challenges our sense of who we are and where we came from. This is why, even though we are inundated with seawater, the advances of our oceanographic agencies do not match those of our space agencies.

He had tracked the family of a senior al-Qaeda commander in Africa to an island off Madagascar. The terrorist's mother lived in a neigh-bourhood on the slopes of a volcano above the island's capital. It was a steep walk up from the town. The air grew thin, there were showers of hail. The massif rose lividly above the shacks. Smoking lines of lava ran down it and were glowing welts at night.

The terrorist was near the top of the FBI's most wanted list. There was a $5 million bounty on his head. He was elusive: the *New York Times* reported him dead on the day of a State of the Union address. The missile was not even close. He moved between Somalia and Kenya on foot, on donkey, in lorries and on dhows. According to the FBI, he was a bomb maker, an expert in urban warfare, a computer hacker, a forger, and a master of disguise who spoke many languages. The bureau could not accept that it was easy to buy a new identity in Kenya and move up and down the Swahili coast and that several languages were spoken there. His information indicated the terrorist was running scared. He thought of the man as an untrained hunter who had wounded an animal and then did not know what to do. He knew he was hidden in Somalia, in rooms where the television played all day, shaping him in new and unexpected ways.

The mother's neighbourhood was filled with music and interspersed with Jurassic-looking trees. Volcanic ash fell on its corrugated iron roofs, lava flowed around it. The people were a Creole particular to that island, descended from runaway slaves and pirates who had landed there. She ran a kiosk a few steps back from the street. It was the kind of shack where most of the world goes each day to buy its milk, tomatoes and sundries. She sat on a stool outside, watching the passers-by. She wore a blue dress and crescent moon earrings. She was not veiled. She looked like she was about to pluck a goose, hands on knees, legs set wide apart. He climbed the steps and asked for a drink. She knew immediately why he was there. He followed her into the shack. She pulled a Coke bottle from a bucket of iced water and opened it for him.

'I'll give you nothing,' she said, refusing to look him in the eye. 'We paid for his education and not a sou did we get. He didn't even turn up for his father's funeral.'

She minded very much being found. He could not remember whether her voice had been rough, or not, only that she had struck him like a character in a fairytale – a cottager in a forest – not someone in a shack on the side of a tropical volcano.

He had zigzagged down to the town, pushing away large moths that brushed his face and stumbled into a courtyard where old men were slapping down dominoes on a wooden table under a swaying street-light. The capital was built with its back to the sea. There were no beaches. The escaped settlers had chosen to face the volcano which sooner or later would spell their doom. There were hardly any animals left on the island. The mongooses had killed the snakes, the people had killed the mongooses. The islanders were ruled by superstitions. There was a miracle mosque that had built itself at night and a crater lake which granted wishes into which a Belgian scuba-diving expedition had gone down and never come back up. There were witches in every village who were paid to cast spells: for a successful visa application to visit France for instance. It was an extreme case of islandism, with no reference to the surrounding ocean. It was as if the rest of the world did not properly exist.

The next day, he remembered, hot ash had fallen on the town and out to sea. Apparently this was quite normal. It was difficult to breathe and the tarmac on the roads bubbled. He met with the terrorist's sister in a café across from a tennis club called Roland Garros, which had beautiful red clay courts. Her name was Monique. She was more forthcoming.

'I don't want money or that,' she said. 'You can buy me breakfast if you like.'

She was a hairdresser. She wore a miniskirt and sunglasses with plastic diamonds glued to the sides.

'The thing about my brother is he's really shy. At least he was,' she corrected herself, 'I haven't seen him in years.'

The volcano was still rumbling under the town. The morning was heavy with languor. She lit a cigarette and inhaled. The magma, the weather, himself; everything felt saved up.

'He was the best student in his class. For some reason the French didn't give him a scholarship. That's how he ended up in Pakistan. If France had come through for him, he'd probably be a maths teacher now.' She sipped her coffee. 'He liked maths. This word terrorist. I don't like it. My brother only fights to support his family. The rest is made up.'

'Your mother says she hasn't had any money from him.'

'Don't listen to a word she says. I bet she was wearing the earrings he sent her.'

'Crescent moons?'

'That's them. He sends money every month. His wife and kids live with me. She gets money transfers too. We're a close family.'

She was unguarded. She even told him which money bureau the terrorist's wife picked the transfers up from.

'Has your brother ever come back to the island?' he asked.

'Course not! The police would have him in a minute. He's gone for good. He's an important man now.'

'Do you find yourself embarrassed to talk about him? He's killed a lot of innocent people.'

She shrugged. 'Why should I be embarrassed? He has his cause. He wants to help the Palestinians. Who else is fighting for them?'

'You said he was fighting for the family.'

'Come on now.'

The French news played on a television. He ordered another coffee and a pastry. It was winter in France. There were blizzards in Auvergne. There was a picture of a ski slope, of snow blowing over a road and sheep huddled by a wall.

'A lot of snow in France this year,' she remarked.

When they came out of the café there were soldiers on the street. They belonged to the national army but looked like French paratroopers, with fatigues tucked into their boots, short-barrelled machine guns on their backs and some wearing mirrored sunglasses. There were no jobs on the island. There were always coups. Another one was on its way.

'You've been very kind,' he said. 'Might I ask one more favour?'

'But of course.'

'I need a haircut. Do you think you could cut my hair?'

'I've never cut gold hair!'

They took a communal taxi across the town. They were squeezed in the back with another woman. He was buttock to buttock between the two. They didn't seem to mind. They were Muslim, but not so religious. Monique rested her hand absently on his knee. They stared at him, and he looked away. Women had rights on the island. They could vote, they could drive cars. The biggest hope was for a grand marriage, which bought entry into the island's aristocracy.

If the terrorist had gone to France, if he had saved up and had a grand marriage, if he had been a maths teacher, if he had invested in Monique's salon, if, if, he would never have blown up the United States Embassy in Nairobi, in an operation al-Qaeda called Kaaba, which killed 212 people and injured 4000 more.

Aziz was giving a clinic in the Bari slum when the fighters broke into the surgery and snatched James. The gap-toothed Saudi, Saif the lion, ordered him to get dressed. He was manhandled down the stairs and hauled into the back of a lorry idling in the street. Saif had been instructed to take some fighters and hide Mr Water in the badlands for a time, then reappear at an agreed spot. It was early in the morning. Kismayo did not stir.

The lorry was a cattle truck, smelling of animals, with benches on either side. A tarpaulin was drawn down over its metal ribs. He was jammed in near the front, between the Chechen who was called Qasab and a Somali boy — small and coiled like a snake — who was unceasingly enraged by real or made up crimes against the body of Islam.

His hands were bound, not his eyes, and so he was able to see the outskirts of Kismayo, framed through the back of the lorry. The exhaust fired, tins of bullets rattled on the metal floor, and the vehicle swayed and slammed on the broken road.

It grew hotter. Donkeys stood in the shade. The lorry turned onto a tarmac road dotted with starving people hobbling to the sea. Sometimes they collapsed on the road, so the fighters had to get down and carry them to the side before continuing. There was no food in the land. The rains had failed again and insecurity had kept the people from harvesting what little they had.

They passed an Italian plantation which had grown tomatoes and bananas for export. That was in the 1960s, when the seaside restaurants in Kismayo, Marka, and Mogadishu were full of customers, the waiters in uniforms, the bands playing, the sea azure, streaked with foamy white, and the pasta always al dente.

The gates into the plantation were broken now and the earth was split and ruined and the Italians were long gone. There was only a man in rags, scratching around under the trees for fallen fruit. When they went by he waved his stick over his head at them slowly and weakly.

The trees in Somalia were festooned in plastic bags of different colours, carried by the wind and snagged on branches. You could work out how many people lived in a settlement by the number of plastic bags on the trees. As they drove on there were fewer and fewer and then there were none. That was how he knew they had left inhabited Somalia behind and rattled into the badlands.

He put his head around the door of the hotel office and asked if he might briefly check his email on the hotel computer. He scanned the messages and then searched for her. He found a homepage on the Imperial College website. She looked younger in the photograph. She was smiling. The page explained her work. The terminology was difficult to follow.

102

At the bottom was a reference to a hydrothermal vent field she had named: the northernmost vent field yet discovered. He read in the online dictionary that 'flinders' described moths as well as shards and that Matthew Flinders was a Royal Naval officer who had circumnavigated Australia for the first time.

He took his morning coffee in the billiards room with the busts. He opened a window and looked out over the parkland. There was a tree whose branches reached down to the snow like an arm. There was a redbrick chimney visible in the woods: early industrial, slender, tapering and long disused. To breathe the clean air, turf, sea, snow, was a luxury after the dirt and jet fuel smog of Africa. There was a mirror in the room and he stood looking at himself; or rather, because he was not vain in that way, he regarded his other self caught inside the mirror.

Darkness, where is its place? In the ocean. In rock. In a passage of caves, for example, newly found in Europe's Moravian karst, some with cathedral-sized chambers 70 metres long, 30 metres wide and 50 metres high.

The end of these chambers has not been reached because an underground river flows too swiftly and deeply to be crossed. The breathing apparatus available to professional cavers is not sufficient. Behind the river, continuing down for kilometres, are chambers which have never been illuminated.

It was what the United States Army called off-grid. It existed on maps and satellite photos, but was without water, so without settlement.

The only tracks were those the camel herders picked out across the pubic scrub of thorn trees and in the wadis.

Saif held up his mobile phones for a clearer reception. He received a final text message before the signal gave out. James saw the screen-saver on one of the phones was of Giggs scoring a goal for Manchester United over and over. Saif passed the phones along to Qasab, who put them in a knapsack together with some hand grenades. The knapsack looked to have been lifted from some long-ago day trip; filled with sandwiches wrapped in paper, cake and a flask of tea.

Saif pulled out a small and finely bound Koran and began to read aloud. Quietly at first, then sonorously. When he was finished he moved down the lorry and squeezed in beside him.

'I want to tell you not to be frightened,' Saif said. 'We are not heading for battle. The jihad has no frontlines. The battle is all around, it is everywhere.'

They had guns, but they were not an army. There was no likeness to the units he had served with. They were skinny men. Apart from Qasab, he had no doubt that all of them would be beaten to death in a confined space by the average British paratrooper. He welcomed the thought.

Nonetheless the jihadists showed their stamina over a longer period. The paratrooper – the Crusader – was stronger and heavier, but grew tired and demoralised more quickly. The paratrooper was limited in his rules of engagement by the need to protect civilians. The paratrooper did not want to die. The jihadists drank water from the ditch and were resigned to the slow rhythm of the insurgency, walking for days in jeans and sandals, shouldering their guns like skis. Some of them sharpened their teeth with metal files. Over time the jihadists might wear down a much larger force. They were the opposite of the United Nations peacekeepers in Africa, who were all logistics and no fight. Those UN

104

outposts were guarded by machine-gun nests, while on the inside the Portakabins were arranged around a mess tent with a television playing one code of football or another, and the only cheer in those places was when a goal was scored, or a try – a ball puncturing a plane. He had been in one remote camp in Sudan and noticed a beautiful half-naked Dinka girl standing at the edge of the tent bathed in the glow of a football match on a television.

There were seventeen fighters in the lorry. They were self-sufficient. They shared with paratroopers only a care for their guns; they were constantly cleaning them. Most did not even own a prayer mat. They were empowered by the prospect of martyrdom. Famines, flash floods, malaria, the bones that were set wrong or not set at all, the hole rotted through the jawbone, the infections, the gamut of psychiatric disorders, all of this assured them that their fate was in every way and in every place an uncertain one, a medieval one. They would not be missed, and no matter that they lacked common sense, information, and adequate equipment, fatalism gave them a durability the paratrooper lacked.

He tried to strike up a conversation with Saif but the road had become rough again and it was hard to make himself understood over the noise. They fell into an uneasy silence.

Somewhere along the way the land just died. It was bleached out and the cracks that were in the soil in the old Italian plantation had here become deep enough to fall into. The insides of these cuts were twisted with roots and there were flints and fossils exposed. The badlands stretched out of sight. He was thirsty. He longed for water.

Rain was coming. They could all feel it, the prospect of it, the weight of it. The light was faded, the clouds were bruised and full. He scratched at his arms with his bound hands until there was a thickness of dirt and skin and blood under his nails. It was the flea bites. The lorry trundled on over the badlands. It rocked him to sleep. When he awoke

105

his mind was fogged. His face hurt and his skin tasted salty. It had not rained.

They stopped the lorry under a canopy of acacia trees. It was late afternoon. He was hauled out. He begged to be allowed to piss. They untied his hands and led him to a bush. An infection had crystallised in him. It was excruciating; it dribbled, there was pus, then a jet. He could smell the camels in a herder's camp nearby. Slow, loping, farting beasts, they smelled like they moved. They tied him to a tree while they set up camp. Qasab was the eldest, then Saif. The rest were boys. They laid out the blankets. The stars began to appear in the sky, hidden by clouds. They seemed to know nothing about camping; how to pick out a sheltered spot, or where to place the fire so the wind would not turn it and smoke them out.

The rain came in the night. It was a downpour so sudden and torrential it had even the most pious fighters shouting curses. The weapons and the blankets were thrown in the back of the lorry. There was not enough room and he was made to lay down under the lorry with some of the fighters. The tarpaulin was ripped and other fighters joined them and then they were lined up together; the sky bright with lightning, there was the closeness of human bodies, the camels could be heard, and Qasab called out a prayer with a hoarse voice. There was a shout. He was dragged out, he stood there, it was hard to see, it was an immersion, then he made out a fighter crouched behind a thorn tree and just on the other side a gazelle kicking in the mud and a lion closing off its nostrils with its paws.

When the rain eased and they were back under the lorry and they could hear the lion feeding he had a strange feeling, which was something like the speed of his passing through the world, hardly stopping, and his understanding that lions had for so many generations taken hoofed animals in the cover of rain in the desert, and that the sound of them in the dark would outlast him and all of his kind, just as even the mud under the lorry would outlast him.

Later, in a hallucinatory lightning strike, he glimpsed another lion coming to the kill. She was gaunt, her tail split, heraldically, the Bohemian way, also bent like the course of his river at home. Someone raised his gun, it was confusing, the prayers, needing to urinate, the engine dripping, the sense of being made of sugar and dissolving, a lantern, a torch, then nothing, a blankness. He saw the fighter taking aim at the lioness and called out: no! Before the trigger was pulled, Saif sprang out from the lorry and kicked the fighter into the mud and kept kicking him. Whether this was discipline or just alpha-male posturing was difficult to say. But the lioness got away.

The night spun on. Mosquitoes moved between their bodies and the drive shaft of the lorry. Each of the whining insects was crimson with blood that might have come from the fighters, from him, from the camels. He felt further from home than he ever had in his life.

What was he? Not an astronaut floating in a void after a spacewalk gone wrong. For all the puddles, not one of her aquanauts. He was an unfortunate spy, tethered to men and boys who wanted to convert or murder him. They had no understanding of where he came from, what was in his head, his country memories; Sassoon memories, a certain tree, a stile, a hedgerow, the flints in the clay of a Yorkshire field; or else, the rest of it, uncontrived, the blur of city life, friendships, faces, the noise and colours streaming in the early hours of a party in Fulham.

These men and boys had gone through the training camps and been made to see a light he could not see. What face? He did not know. Mohammedanism was without a face.

He was not wholly unsympathetic. He had read the Koran. He supported the Palestinians, mostly, as did many in the secret intelligence service. He had gone on foot through hostile country for days to reach the minaret of Jam in Afghanistan. The beauty of it had moved him to tears. His views were conventional: he was set against appeasement. The Muslim world had to allow laboratories and churches to be built. There should be a compulsory reading from Voltaire in every madrasa.

107

Gay bars and nudist beaches on the Saudi Riviera could wait. Whatever words he might speak under the weight of his captivity, he was an unbeliever. These men of Islam held up a sword with a Koran. That was their strength; that was what made them abhorrent to him.

The drizzle continued through the night and the next day winged termites rose from within the earth in great numbers. He was leaned against the side of the lorry, and the droplets fell softly on his face, with no more force than a tear. Through the campfire the droplets fell, through the growing light, causing termites to glitter. Falling in such a way that it became bewitching. It was little wonder the Musulman was consumed with the idea of paradise as a garden on which rain fell softly. It seemed irrelevant whether paradise was on this planet, or in another place entirely, but the rain was important.

The grass, the thorns, the floor of the encampment and the bed of the lorry were silvered with tens of thousands of termite wings. Grounded, without sight, the termites trembled and died in silence, not deafeningly like bees; without protest, one alone from the other. He watched them and made himself believe that their only flight produced in them an ecstasy which their body had evolved to receive and magnify and that, at the moment their wings peeled off, the quivering height of their creation was not laughter or speech, but a single sustained orgasm. Some of the fighters went around the camp picking up the termites and fried them for breakfast. He was given flat bread like a pitta, filled with them. He bit into it. There was a crunch, then juices.

He was allowed to walk with Saif in the morning and together they found the remains of the kill the lion had made.

'A lioness and cubs,' he said. 'You saved them.'

'Our fight is elsewhere,' Saif said, dismissively.

The sun shone. The fighters dried themselves and their possessions and their guns. They were less bedraggled and looked cleaner than before the rain.

108

When the camel herders left they went by the camp and shouted obscenities. He did not know what, but it was brazen. The herders were wild men, the kind who used to castrate their enemies and use their genitals for snuff pouches. Several of the younger boys ran out after them. The herders turned and shouted more abuse and spat through closed teeth like cats. One of them pulled down his gun, the other ran for cover. Shots were fired. The herder with the gun dropped dead. They chased the other herder and shot him through the shoulder blades. He fell down into the brush.

James was tied to a boy. The boy ran and he ran with him. The other fighters were already crowded around. The herder was on his knees. The exit wound was small. All the jihadists watched him die without looking away. James did also. The herder crawled forward. His lungs were punctured. Blood puffed into the air with his every breath.

'They were going to report our position,' Qasab said, in Arabic. 'They had to be killed.'

It was Qasab who butchered the camel calf, then let the other camels go.

They drove down into a wadi, such as he had seen Yusuf standing in, his arms sunk in the jar of spermaceti.

It was slow going. At some points they all had to jump down and walk beside the lorry, removing the boulders blocking the way, while Saif checked their position on a GPS. The mosquitoes rose hungrily from strips of filthy water. At points the wadi widened into a ravine. The lorry ground on over olivine basalt polished by the hoofs of camels gone before them. They halted under a tree whose trunk and branches were butter yellow. The lorry shone in the shade, shone all the way to space, to the American satellite they had taken their coordinates from, or so Saif thought. He was scared of being spied on more than anything else, and decided that they should stop there, camouflage the lorry, and continue on after sunset; stupid, because the satellites or Reaper drones with their thermal indicators were more likely to spot a lorry moving at night than in the day.

They took the munitions out of the lorry and kept their distance, in case it was taken out in an air strike.

Later, they gave him a plate of camel meat and rice and tea. The water was from a hole they had dug in the riverbed. It was not syrupy like the tea the others drank. He was beaten for refusing to collect firewood. It was part of his plan. By being selectively uncooperative, he could win favour by being unexpectedly cooperative.

'Everyone else is already here,' she whispered.

It was a formal dinner. Her dress shimmered purple and brown and in and out of those colours, showing off her breasts and hips. She took his arm as they went in. He was uncomfortable. He doubted he would have gone by himself. He hated regimental dinners and balls.

It snowed so heavily that the staff had to sweep it from the roof; so heavily that it transformed Bethlehem in his mind from a grubby little Palestinian town despoiled by Israel into a proper French country town; the shepherds in the snowy fields, the angels above.

She wore a silver Ethiopian cross that glinted in the candlelight. They were seated at the table at which Ibsen had eaten his goose in Christmas 1899. They took that as a foretoken of happy times.

Joyeux Noël! Peace and goodwill, hot chocolate and furs, and every phone switched off, please. There was a Nativity play, madrigals, some Haydn on a trumpet, an unidentifiable piano piece. The waiters wore tailcoats. Lifting a finger to them was considered gauche; they acknowledged the slightest nod, and glided out of the kitchen like a Greek chorus.

Between them, over the course of the evening, they ate servings of duck foie gras with a peach wine jelly, Scottish scallops, ham, deboned saddle of lamb from the Auvergne, white beans with truffles, sea bream, poached apricots, bay leaf panacotta, cheeses and chocolates. They drank champagne, a house white wine, Rothschild Bordeaux, Chateau Villefranche dessert wine; he an espresso and she a cup of rooibos tea. There were also almonds and Christmas pudding with brandy sauce from the Ritz in London.

He wore a blue suit with suede shoes and a grey Turnbull & Asser shirt. He had only his regimental cufflinks with him. A silver parachute on maroon. He did not think she would notice.

He was in many ways old-fashioned. He envied Victorian explorers for having such obvious goals and for the contrast they experienced between the world they discovered and the world they returned to. Nothing was that clearly defined any more. He did not trust emotions. He trusted knowledge and duty. Yes, duty. His work was only occasionally terrifying. When it was he dealt with it. His mind was supple, the mind of a future head of intelligence, who believed the greatest service he could offer in the complicated present was to help people catch up emotionally with where they stood historically. They were almost exactly coeval.

'You were in the army,' she said.

'What makes you say that?'

'Just about everything. Those cufflinks for a start. The tattoo. I've never met a man who folds his clothes and arranges his shoes before getting into bed.'

'It was a long time ago,' he said. 'A short service commission.'

'You sound like you regret it.'

'In some ways.'

'You jumped out of planes?'

'Yes, I jumped.'

'Wow!' she said, echoing his wow. She wasn't French, not really. Of course she saw his cufflinks, of course she saw through him. It would be only a little while before the nature of his spying was similarly evident; the lies, thefts, deaths; the despots of the agency, the good men and women who were prevented from getting out.

She did not ask him what it was like to jump out of a plane, she did not say: what was it about the army you didn't like? She said, 'Can I say something in German? Would you mind?'

'Not at all,' he said. Then, 'I don't speak German.'

'Just listen to the words.'

She spoke them slowly and clearly:

'*Durch den sich Vögel werfen, ist nicht der vertaute Raun, der did Gestacht dir steigert.*'

'Something about a bird.'

'It's Rilke. What birds plunge through is not the inner space in which you see all forms intensified. I thought it might mean something to a paratrooper.'

He was noncommittal. 'I haven't jumped in years.'

They talked about supermodels, punk, and the King's Road.

She talked about her nephew, Bertrand, Bert.

There was so much they could not talk about. She could not simplify the maths for him. He was legally bound to hide behind a false identity. They talked cheerfully of Christmas things and listened to the madrigals and only when the meats arrived, the waiters hastening like star-led wizards with odours sweet, did she ask him about Africa.

'Tell me about French Africa.'

'Djibouti,' he answered, without thinking.

'Where's Djibouti?'

'Between Eritrea and Somaliland.'

She nodded.

'It looks the way lots of places are going to look. The capital is Djibouti Ville. It's dilapidated. The main square has been renamed, but everyone still calls it by its colonial name. The speakeasies where the French legionnaires drink are sandbagged against suicide bomb attacks, although the prostitutes show off their wares all the same. The shops directly off the main square are run by Chinese traders. The presidential helicopter flies low over the market stalls in the evenings.

112

Everyone has a mobile phone with a camera and music player built in. Many of the Djiboutian men forget to turn them off when they enter into the mosque, so the prayers are interrupted by a mix of ring tones, some of them religious, more often theme tunes, or French hip-hop. The camels are driven in from the desert in the early evening to be butchered and you can sometimes see the Afaris hacking away at the camel hump then gathering around to drink from the green mess there, just as they've done for hundreds of years. The buildings are often rubble and where they are not are plastered with adverts for toothpaste and soap. It's such a hot place, there is not even breeze out on the harbour, and I can't tell you what's in the water there, it never occurred to me before I met you, there are whale sharks in the Gulf of Tadjoura I think, and volcanoes along the shore. It's very geologically active.'

'Is it French?'

'Only in the Foreign Legion camps and sometimes in the harbour you can see one of those old French tramp steamers headed for Reunion and on to Calédonie. At the same time, Tarek bin Laden, who's a brother of Osama bin Laden, wants to build the world's longest bridge between Djibouti and Yemen across the Bab el-Mandeb, the Gate of Tears, and he wants to construct cities on either side of the bridge as a hope for humanity. There will be a city for two million people in Djibouti and a city for four million people in Yemen. The projected cost is $40 billion and the start-up work is being handled by American defence contractors, with the full backing of the CIA.'

He stopped. He had strayed alarmingly into his real work: he had been seconded to look into the bridge project.

'That's interesting about the crossing. According to the evidence, genetic and archaeological, irrefutable, I'd say, but I don't want to rain on anyone's parade, every non-African in the world is descended from a band of thirty or so humans who made it across the Gate of Tears some 60,000 years ago, walking and wading and perhaps on rafts from Africa to Arabia. We're all African. Nearly all of our genetic diversity

113

is within us, not between races. Given a similar history of migration, any African tribe will turn blond and blue-eyed. We become curdy in France and black in the sun. We've already escaped once as a species. We made it out of your Rift Valley to Somalia and then to the Middle East. There were no more than a few thousand of us left alive.'

'That's all? I can't believe it. We must have been outnumbered at every watering hole by monkeys.'

'What this means, genetically, is that every living person who is not African is a descendant of one of those individuals who crossed the Red Sea, while every African is a descendant of those who stayed, give or take some mixing.' She pointed at herself, as if to say voila! 'This explains the genetic diversity in Africa, where a villager may be further removed from his neighbour than you are from a Polynesian. This is exodus.'

She turned towards the pianist who was then playing French carols softly. He was certain that at some point in his life he would look back on this evening, at her.

'What is it?'

He held her gaze. 'Nothing.' It was everything. He saw in her one possible future. Her skin, her facial features. Then again it was not so new; the febrile order of races was breaking down long before.

The evening went more slowly then, like a stone sinking into a lake. They were tired and more cosy in their tiredness, and as so often happens in long dinners, their conversation became haunting.

He started it by taking a sip of his dessert wine and telling of how, in 1597, the poet John Donne set sail to the Azores with the Earl of Essex to intercept a Spanish treasure fleet in Angra Bay on Teceira Island, with its mild climate, plentiful wood and orchards, and fields to fatten the cattle left by the sailors on their outbound voyage to the New World.

'Donne was still a lusty mate on Essex's adventure, a poet,' he said, 'but on his return to England he renounced the fugitive life to become

a clergyman. In that capacity he tremendously ministered to his congre-
gants. His sermons and meditations minister still.'

'"No man is an island entire of itself",' he recited, '"every man is
a piece of the Continent, a part of the main; if a clod be washed away
by the sea, Europe is the less."'

'What do you think happens,' he added, on his own account, 'to
bodies buried at sea?'

'I've never given it much thought,' she said, falsely. 'It's not dust to
dust, that's for sure, it's water to water. We're made of water, it's the
most obvious thing, still we don't get it, we think we're solid, we're
not, we're pockets of moisture. We bleed. Our mouths, our eyes, our
every opening to the air are filled with saliva, mucus, or wax. If we
were too long in the sun we should soon dry up.'

'It is a shock to be a jelly,' he said, lighting a cigarette. 'Are we
allowed to smoke?'

'I think so.'

'If man is made of water, does that follow that angels are made of
air?'

'Angels are made of light. What made you think of that?'

'Haven't you noticed there are angels everywhere in the hotel? They're
above the entrance, in the mirror hall, on the stairs. Donne said that
angels do not propagate or multiply. That they were made at first in
abundance and so were stars. That raises a problem. The human
population is exploding, yet the number of angels stays the same.'

'You're worried we'll get lonely and won't have anyone to show us
the way?'

'It's what you were saying yesterday. Everything will be quantified
and there will be less of everything.'

'It's not complicated,' she said, her voice ever so slightly changed.
'Suppose there is a god, a big suppose, suppose he's all knowing, well,
he'll know before he begins what the maximum human population
on earth and in the universe will be. Since he's all powerful he'll run
the programme so that x number angels, a trillion angels, enter

existence sometime after the big bang, but he'll make them unconscious, not quite born, until they have someone to look after. It's just as likely newborns are awakening angels.'

'You don't believe?'

'You do?'

'I do,' he said. 'And I'm not sorry for saying so.'

She could have pulled back at this point, from credulity, but when you are drawn to someone there are things you cannot share that come with them too. Besides, she had her own experiences, her own imaginings.

She looked at him directly. 'I have a problem believing in anything that can't evolve,' she said. 'What makes Donne an authority anyway?'

He thought for a moment. 'Generosity? Awareness?' Another line of Donne's came to him. '"But I do nothing upon myself and yet I am my own executioner."'

'Do you know why in paintings you never see angels smile?'

'No.'

'Because they're so ancient.'

Her work had given her a sense of the importance of imagination. It interested her that angels predated the surviving religions, and with a fineness of detail. Angels were not superheroes. They had no humours. They were flawless, inhuman. She saw a Babylonian clay box and kneeling in it a furled angel. If she lifted a lantern to it, as if adjusting a spotlight on a submersible, she would be able to see clearly the anatomy of its back and shoulders. The angel would stand, giant in her consciousness, its head bent down. She would stare up into its meteor-scarred face and its wings would open slowly, with pinguid plumage, a wider span than any sea eagle. Then the angel would get down again in the box and she would walk away, back into her own life, London, work, bills.

'Tell me something horrible,' she said.

'Why would I do that? "Tis the season to be jolly."'

'We don't have much time. Is that a reason?'

116

He was quiet. 'It would turn your stomach.'

'My stomach is strong enough.'

His mind raced. He was not a water engineer. He had seen violence. He had done it.

'OK,' he said, finally. 'Another death rite. Do you remember the Luos I told you about in the forest in Nairobi?'

'The hyenas digging them up? Barack Obama's people?'

'That's it. Most of them live in Western Kenya, on the shores of Lake Victoria. The isolated fishing villages there still hold to traditions codified before independence in a pamphlet called the *Luo kiti gi tubege*. I've read it, so I'm certain that what I saw in one of the villages there was not an aberrance. A boy drowned in the reeds where the women wash clothes and the crocodiles are hidden. He was a hunchback. He was weak, the people said, and he had had difficulty walking. Before he could be buried, his hunch had to be opened. His family paid a man in goats to do the job. The price used to be paid in cows, but no one can afford a cow. The lake is fished out and the people are penniless.

'Everyone in the village gathered around,' he said. 'The man sharpened his axe. I thought I was watching an execution. Then I saw the corpse laid face down on a string bed so the hunch was exposed. There was sadness, also tension; if the man made a mistake, the hunch would pass to his family. If he made no mistake, the lake would take the curse. The man drank banana wine and swung the axe about, loosening up. He ran his hands up and down the boy's spine, searching for the spot, his hand bumped along. Finally he stood over the corpse and tapped at the point of the hunch with the axe and opened it up.'

'I've seen nothing with my own eyes,' she said, after a silence had passed between them. 'Only the news.'

He gave a querying look.

'Since I was a child,' she said, 'I've pictured a slave ship sinking during an Atlantic crossing.'

'A dream?'

'No. A series of lithographs. Slightly different faces each time. Very close up, often at strange angles. It begins the same way. The boatswain is fumigating the slave hold with a red-hot chain dipped in a bucket of tar. The chain is too hot. He drops it on the varnished deck. The decking bursts into flames. The helmsman abandons the wheel. Sailors suffocate in the smoke. The varnish bubbles. The slaves are screaming below decks. I seldom see them. When I do, it always unclear, very black, just the suggestion of an open mouth, the glint of metal. The sailors let down the rowing boats. They do not ever think to let go the slaves. Water pours in. The ship breaks up and disappears under the waves. Do you know what I see next?'

'I can't guess.'

'Nothing. Just the surface of the sea. It's my non-existence. My slave ancestor is drowned in the Atlantic and I'm never born.'

'The Australian side of your family will be fine.'

'Until the convict transport goes down,' she said, putting on an Australian accent. 'There's some part of me,' she went on, 'that thinks I became interested in the ocean to see where those slaves went, how deep they sank. Recently the images are further and further from the ship. You cannot make out the faces, only the shapes of the sailors, the ship catching light and breaking apart. Several times now I've dreamt that I am leafing through the lithographs on the platform of a train station in what I remember to be Argentina. There's a wide river, a plain, vineyards, then snowcapped mountains, Bariloche. It's always autumn, the leaves stick like stamps to the platform, and I am told the story of the slave ship in great detail by an elderly man, who is sitting on a bench next to me.'

They were each gifted a small Christmas present. She received a small crystal rabbit; he a camping knife. A glass of whisky arrived for him.

He was in that mood when he thought of the metaphysical. He was closer to Donne than to Ibsen. Heaven was like being tuned out. You entered in and were suffused in an equal light, without sun or storms, never atmospheric, and were met also by one equal sound.

Somalia is not the Africa that is known. You will never see a naked man there. Everyone is shrouded, covered up. There are no nomads shouldering crates of Coca-Cola with scarification on their cheeks and chests; no swinging thin cocks.

And it should be said that the coming of age initiations of jihadists in Somalia are not anywhere near so demanding as the circumcision ceremony of Masai boys, who are disowned if they flinch when a sharp knife is drawn around the head, and are rewarded with girls wearing necklaces on their chest, safety pins in their skin, smelling of earth, of goats, their buttocks daubed with ochre paste, their breasts firm, with unsuckled nipples, if they remain expressionless. The Masai boy circumcised in silence has access to the milk and blood of the cattle, a knife of his own and a spear. Whatever his creed, he will sing and jump in the Masai way. If he does not go to the city and become lost there he will be strong enough to walk for days barefoot and to keep walking into his old age long after his eyesight and hearing fail him.

The lot of the mujahid is in some ways easier, in others harder. It is easier to pull a trigger or push the remote-control button on an improvised explosive device (mobile phones are unreliable) than it is to suffer a knife without anaesthetic and give no sign of pain. On the other hand, the endurance of a jihadist has no obvious reward in this life.

They walked along the wadi at night, the lorry following at a distance. They slept at dawn. The wind came in the afternoon, when they packed their camp. The wadi was a crack in the earth made by water and abandoned by water and it funnelled the wind so that even when they wrapped their faces they could hardly see for dust. He drank from the greasy ribbons and became more ill. He vomited the food he was given and meandered like an Englishman at the midday hour and no one stopped him because there was nowhere to go. He wandered too far and was caught and bound hand to foot. He could crawl to a crevice and urinate there. For the other he needed to be untied.

Heat prickled under his scalp. The snakes did not move from under the rocks. Neither did the jihadists. He fell over his own shadow. He had been one of those paratroopers who could kill a fighter with his bare hands. Now he could not keep up with them. He was built for structures and systems. In his stupors he saw the sun harden and arc across the sky and soften in the evening. There were the colours of petrified wood. He heard prayers in the shade. If he could only climb out of the wadi he would get onto the world.

When his mind and breathing were clear and sober he saw that the wadi was divided between the parts where sunlight struck and the parts where it never reached. These parts were a reminder of what Danny had said, that the strangest life exists in the cracks.

He thought in future times the great literature would be translated into a hieroglyphic script based on hexagonal forms, including that passage in *Utopia* where his saintly ancestor dreamt up vast deserts of the equator

parched with the heat of the sun, the soil was withered, all things looked dismally, and all places were either quite uninha-bited, or abounded with wild beasts and serpents, and some few men, that were neither less wild nor less cruel than the beasts themselves.

The light and dark in the wadi helped him to better understand the jihadist worldview.

'What is the influence of the desert on Islam?' he asked Saif, when he was feeling better.

'What do you mean?' Saif said. 'The desert is also true for the Christians. Jesus went to the desert.'

He knew the damp in England's bones. 'Not any more,' he said. 'Not in England.'

He believed the contrast in the desert helped create the Abrahamic religions and the advance and enlightenment of Christendom was an admittance of rainy days and nights. It came back to the weather. The clouds that covered up the stars in England, the seasons of drizzle there, the mists, the storms, the trees losing their leaves, all of it made a mockery of Bedouin absolutes.

There were slender trees in the wadi, very old, hard as rock, and in their dusky hollows and roots were spiders and mice.

One night when they were walking they came across a cormorant too weak to fly. It sat on the rock flapping its wings, like a goose in a farmyard. If it rained the cormorant would survive, but there was no sign of more rain.

He thought about sex a lot while he walked. Not the rutting of pastoralists, not the pent-up sexual desire of the fighters; he put himself instead somewhat comically on the dance-floor in Kampala, the suck of it, a fountain of Ugandan women's arses, gyrating, pumping, and wiggling huge breasts; the mirrors, cigarettes, bottles of Nile beer, cheap Chinese furnishings, the sweat; and all the other men at the far end of the dance-floor watching an English football match on the television, leaving him alone to satisfy all the women, each of them in turn presenting themselves, which, trudging along, he had no difficulty in doing.

There was once a Hungarian count from Transylvania who sold a family diamond to fund an expedition to east Africa. His porters called him fatty.

He bought his guns from Holland & Holland in London and recovered some of the costs of his expedition with the sale of ivory from the elephants he shot; the ivory which many of the piano keys in Vienna of that period were fashioned.

One of the count's contemporaries, a young American braggart, was said to have taken several pairs of flesh-coloured gloves when he went overland to the Tina River, with the intention of making the Somalis think he was peeling the skin off his hands, although that is hard to credit. Would the Somalis ever have fallen for it?

It was easier to take if Africa was doing it to him. Africa was a rough mistress to pale men. If he considered his captivity in this way he could place his journey at the undistinguished end of African exploration; nothing more than an outing. He thought badly of many of the white explorers and white hunters, because of their violent acquisitiveness. He believed in being of service to others. If he had been more gentle, he really could have been Mr Water.

The grass was tall by the lakes in Congo and the mud there was so heavy on his boots at the end of the day it could not be stamped off and had be removed with a knife or a spoon. There was maize growing in the shambas, also squash, cassava, spinach, peas, groundnuts, sometimes guava, mango, watermelon and many types of banana; stewed, and served with shreds of chicken or tilapia. The villagers hung beehives in the trees for the wild bees to colonise. These hives were barrels, fashioned of bamboo strips, and covered in mud, dung and leaves. One end was sealed with banana bark, the other netted with vines and twine. He thought of workers on the slopes of the volcanoes above the lakes. Walking home on wet paths through fields of sorghum whose red tassels swayed, hoes on their shoulders, alongside clear-flowing streams; each worker to their windowless mud huts with roofs of terracotta tiles.

He thought of the mattered water of the lakes, their rock formations and the old steamer ships fallen on their sides on the shore. Of the bars on the Congolese side – the Zebra bar and the Sir Alex bar – and the soldiers leaving, stumbling out of them in the early morning, still in wellington boots, still armed, taking with them girls pushed by their families to sleep with them in the hope of securing better rations and protection.

He thought especially of the thundering afternoon rain, a child selling tomatoes one by one at the roadside through the downpour, the steaming land that followed, the monkeys sprinting up the trees, and a man sitting on a stool outside his hut, reading the Bible in the last light of the day.

There was a town on a lake between Congo and Rwanda where the wind blew stiffly, but produced no waves. There was a Soviet-built hospital on the hill of the town and a beacon behind it which brightened in the dusk, and there was a boy selling sticks of chewing gum who, as he ambled by, glanced at the sky and said: 'Look! The moon is taking the light away from the sun.'

They drove up out of the wadi. It was Martian, but there was movement; impala springing away, rock pythons and poisonous frogs. They passed a grave where the body was laid above the ground with stones piled on it. The headstone commended a herder's life to the Almighty. There were a few wild people who paid them no attention, but took shelter from the sun and the wind in round huts made of paper, plastic and cloth.

They arrived at a place no satellite image can do justice to. There was a plain of volcanic clinker, like on the slopes of the terrorist's island, then the lorry drove down below sea level onto a Greenlandic whiteness. Even close up it had the look of pack ice, with those same veins of green. All the shades of white were visible and there were roseate floes far out to sea. It crunched under their feet when they jumped down onto it. But it was illusory. It was not the life-giving ice of the north that melts and freezes, under which the beluga whale swims. It was a salt flat. The mists were chlorine vapours. There were no birds in the sky. It was littered with the bones of animals which had strayed there and died and been covered in salt. He picked up what he took to be the skull of a gazelle. It looked frozen, the sockets hoary, but the salt broke apart at the slightest touch, leaving only the bone.

Saif ordered the group to smash up slabs of salt and load them onto the lorry that they might trade later in their journey for charcoal and whey. He helped wrap them in sisal. He brushed salt from his hair and face. It formed on all of them. They began to look frosted to each other: it was impossible to live under the rim of the world.

The ground was flat as a billiard table. It had been underwater in the last pluvial period. When he looked more carefully he saw the scattered teeth of prehistoric fish and crocodiles.

The arrival of a soul in heaven is like a sailing ship discovering the harbour whereunto it saileth. But the truth of Danny's voyage was that she sailed to no harbour. They had left Iceland behind, Akureyri, with its fjord and green hills and glaciers, and steamed north into the Greenland Sea, Grønlandshavet. She was bound for the largest uncharted hydrothermal vent field in the world, far below the plunging icebergs and the blue-black top, in a part of the Hadal deep whose unlit clock ticked at an incalculably slower speed.

It was the most important summer cruise she had been on. It held the chance, she believed, to reckon the extent of life in the fissures of the rock underlaying the Hadal deep. She had been one of those who discovered the vent field the previous summer. She had been asked to name it and had called it the Enki field.

She was aboard the French oceanographic research vessel *Pourquoi Pas?* which carried also the French Navy submersible, *Nautile*. The preparations had gone well. Her lab equipment was in place. Thumbs was along for the ride. The scientists were French, British, German, Swiss, Italian and Norwegian. She was inclined to stereotype nationalities. There were enough Brits to guarantee showings of *Monty Python's Flying Circus* in the evenings. The French, she thought, would take care of wine at meals and hand around cigarettes on deck. The Italians would surprise. She was happy anyway not to be on an American boat. The Americans were more self-congratulatory, with less bon viveurs, with people in the fluorescent-lit galley reading airport novels, sipping iced water through the evenings. There was a pressure on American boats to purchase ugly expedition T-shirts, even sweatshirts, as if a badge was needed to prove that you had touched the ocean and partaken in your own profession. She refused to buy the items. Even when she was given them she never wore them, except for a cap. She offended those American women who habitually covered themselves in such loose-hanging cotton garbs, who seldom wore high heels in their lives, and who felt she was a snob and an ice maiden.

She was a snob. She detested what was vulgar; vulgarity was something else. Thumbs had it best when he said she was two cats in one: a Persian and an alley cat. For inasmuch as she dressed carefully and stylishly on the boat, and expended her mind in the lab, she had drunk, punched and screwed her way through science cruises over the years with a dirtiness beyond the suspicions of her detractors.

They rattled up into the green hills.

'We're going to where the water is,' said one of the boys.

His Somali was improving; he understood.

In the clouds there was a hut tended by a shepherd in a ski jacket. Geese flew overhead and one of the fighters covered his ears to their honking. There was grazing. Water trickled from the rock into a pool green with algae.

It was easier out of the heat. Even the mad boy, the snake, became more reasonable and did not strike so often. Down there in the badlands were those who did not know any more where to dig for water, and so tied up a cow to the point of death, then cut its rope and let it go smell the water out.

The shepherd made extra money by harvesting frankincense. It was not clear whether his connection with Yusuf was related to that trade, or whether they shared a shepherding past, but the nicks in the boswellia trees, and how carefully the shepherd attended them, stood in contrast to the boiling down of a whale for perfume.

The hut had two rooms with a cement floor. The doors and windows were gone and there was a thickness of dust and dead flies throughout, but he could picture a Calabrian shepherd once hiding out here to escape the law. It must have been an Italian who planted the cypress tree at the back of the property. It was tall and cast a tapering shadow up the hillside. James would not have believed a cypress could have so prospered there, but it was well planted, in a shady spot.

It was different from the coast. The wind ripped through in the mornings, and there was a stillness at the end of the day: the land seemed to sigh with the fleeing light.

It was a new, soft, blown-apart hill. The spring water attracted all kinds of thirsty animals. There were dik-diks, of course. They made only the slightest disturbance, their tiny hoofs staying a second in the

126

dust. Three elephants walked through. They had climbed the hill for a drink. They moved cautiously, snapping the branches. They were small, with short tusks. It was improbable, yet that was how nature was. Hippos appeared at waterholes from nowhere. Tilapia fish eggs attached themselves to the legs of water birds and spread from one pool to another. Life clung to life.

James had met an old Serbian poet in New York City. The man was always living hand to mouth, on the edge, and bitter that his Yugoslav neighbourhood had turned Haitian.

There was a basketball court beside his tenement where the youths came to play.

'Cocksucking blacks. They shout. They're rude, you know. I'd whip them with my fists . . . But look at me, I'm so old I want to go to church, know what I mean?'

What sounded like vot. W was a *v*, t was sometimes *tz*.

It was a small room. The man gave him a glass of clear alcohol and told him about observing the faces of Ustashe soldiers during the Second World War, even though James had come to him on a matter related to the Balkan wars of the 1990s.

The poet said that as a young man he was standing off to one side under an oak tree on an October day.

'It couldn't have been November, no, it was October, you know, it was one of those days that ain't summer and ain't winter, with mush-rooms, with berries. When the Ustashe was shot there was a kind of a cloud from their face, you know, or it was from the back of the head, yeh, like a breath, yeh. I remember the ground was wet, my boots were wet. It wasn't warm. It was in the mountains, around Plitvice.'

The poet had left Yugoslavia in 1960; his poems in exile had made him a figurehead for some Serbian paramilitaries.

127

'It came I couldn't stand Tito. He sold us out. Anyway, I was brought forward, I was asked to shoot one of these Ustashe in the head. I couldn't do it. I mean, I could think about doing it any number of times, yes, but a real gun, a real man, uh-uh.'

There was the screeching of the last elevated train, the Jamaica line, the poet said, then a single bird on the street outside, then nothing; the basketball court was empty. There was an open notebook on the table and a sharpened pencil.

'It's funny,' the poet said, 'how things go around in your mind. Whirligigs they call them, in them toy shops uptown. Here I am in New York City, but I ain't in New York. I was born in a kingdom, the KINGDOM of Serbs, Croats and Slovenes. Yes, I seen a war, I come to America, how to explain, I float, the baseball seasons come, they finish, the snow comes, goes, never money, but time is standing still for me, like I was every day stamping a time clock.'

He threw his hands in the air. His body language was all New York.

'You come ask me about the future. These men in hiding. This Bosnia. What do I know, I'm the wrong guy, I just can't move.'

According to the Koran, Allah created angels from light, then created jinn from smokeless flame. Man was made of clay and breathed into only when the jinn disappointed Allah by climbing to the top of the sky and eavesdropping on the angels there. But Allah did drown the jinn or otherwise destroy them. He allowed them all to live in parallel, coexisting in the world.

It is possible for jinn to see men and take possession of their bodies. It is more difficult for men to see jinn; their country is oblique to ours. In certain traditions, anyone who glimpses the real face of a jinn dies of fright.

There are a few telltale signs of jinn among us. In the eyes and speech patterns, or in the feet, which are often set backwards. Jinn have a freedom of choice like man does. They can choose to believe or not, to be good or bad. 'And among us jinn there are those who are righteous and those who are far from that. We are sects, having different rules,' says the Koran.

The weapons against malign jinn are religious certitude and education, both of which produce a roaring of thought that the jinn cannot stand. So those jinn who choose to step into our country prefer to occupy bodies which are in a liminal state: a menstruating or pregnant woman, a lunatic, someone incoherent with anger, or a man and a woman having sex, when consciousness is a sheet of copper beaten down, mirroring only the moment.

The serpent in the Garden of Eden is said to be a shape-shifting jinn. They are blamed for the manias of the night. There is no agreement among Muslim clerics on whether jinn are physical or subtle. Some clerical accounts have them as giant and hideously ursine, with matted hair, long yellow teeth; they are the abominable snowmen of the Hindu Kush and the Himalaya. This kind of jinn can be slain with plum pips or other fruit stones fired from a sling. Scholarly clerics prefer to describe jinn as an energy, perhaps a pulse responsive to the laws of physics, which are alive at the margins of sleep or madness, and expand themselves into other semiconscious states of existence. An extension of this thinking is that jinn are the continuance of thoughts that were in the world before man.

He was no closer to Saif. He did not care for the man's gap teeth, his outbursts, and he was determined also to avoid any suggestion of Stockholm syndrome, in which the captive develops an affection for his captor. Yet when they cooked legs of mutton, it was Saif who made sure he ate, and gave him tea. It was Saif who came and spoke to him.

They sat together and looked out over Somalia. In the day it was possible to see all the way to the salt flats, but at night all of this disappeared to a blankness, with no lights at all.

He was marched with Saif and the foreigners to a cave at the top of a hill. Saif insisted on walking into the cave. The other fighters were too frightened to follow.

'Come with me,' Saif said to him.

So he went inside too.

There was a pit in the centre of the cave.

'It goes all the way to hell,' Saif whispered.

They got down on their bellies and inched their way to the edge. Saif threw a stone in and it was lost, there was no sound of it at all.

'Let us see,' Saif said.

A coolness flowed up from it. Somewhere in the earth's mantle, or in another province of existence, or present in one of the diatoms on the walls, Saif believed, was a city of jinn. James saw a glistening in the pit, water dripping, or perhaps something else. What would happen if he threw himself in? In what part of the world would he find himself? As soon as he thought this he was overcome with dizziness. Saif, for his part, was shaking uncontrollably. Without a word to one another, they crawled back.

The fear that most often accompanies the presence of jinn is the fear of losing the faculty of reason. That is exactly what he felt; the rock giving way under him, something trying to pick him up and twirl him in the air. There were voices, movements. He was frightened and yet curiously happy, because the fear did not belong to his captivity.

Saif tried to say a prayer aloud at the cave entrance, but stumbled on the words and did not finish the last verse. The other fighters were shouting further down the hill. They had convinced themselves jinn were scavenging bones around them. Saif took the safety off his gun and ran down the hill. He followed; it was a moment when he was the same as Saif, sharing the same uncertainty.

*

Saif believed in jinn. The CIA was a jinn agency. So was James's true employer. There were also righteous jinn, Saif said, who whispered into the breasts of those about to die in battle.

'You know, Water, the Jews control jinn,' Saif said, the next day.

'How is that?'

'It has always been so. You think Jews gain wealth and power through work alone? No, no. Solomon himself used jinn to build up the temple in Jerusalem. If you were ever to find a lamp in which a jinn is trapped, you will see that the magic spell on the lamp is written in Hebrew, yes, not Arabic.'

If jinn were manifestations of thoughts that were in the world before the existence of man – ursine, monstrous to behold – what would the creatures of the thoughts left by man look like?

He made love to her in his room. He placed her on her knees on the Turcoman rug. She was heaved forward, holding onto nothing.

It was his last night at the Hotel Atlantic. He insisted she share his bed. She fell asleep in his arms immediately. The weight of her was on his chest. He could not sleep – it was the food, the caffeine, also the taking leave – and as he lay there, in spite of the Christmas cheer and the sinking of the evening to the slave ship, he could not get out of his mind his own body, how his muscles were only holding in liquids.

They lay in bed all morning. She rode him rhythmically. She felt run through, defeated; the turning that had thrown them together was about to pull them apart. It was a hotel. You came, you left.

'I'll swim in the sea this afternoon,' she said, when she was dressing.

'Not by yourself.'

131

'I'm strong. I'll to keep to the shore.' She hesitated, she was nervous. 'What if I came to visit you in Nairobi?'

'Don't say it if you don't mean it,' he said. He smiled, but at the same time he was thinking, she can't. 'I'll take you to Lamu.'

'I want to swim in your pool.'

He left after lunch. He was meant to catch the evening Eurostar from Paris to Leeds. The same taxi driver was waiting for him. The same Mercedes.

She stood on the steps. The sign spelling Hotel Atlantic looked suddenly clownish. She was a stranger to him. He did not know her. Everything was running in reverse, the opposite of when they met on the beach. The sun broke through the clouds in such a way that even the snow appeared to drift up. He was walking backwards down the steps. Then something strange happened to the light, the colours shifted, the parkland went blue, and she walked down the steps and put her arms around him and he kissed her tenderly on the lips and they understood they were in love. He knew her, had known her, would know her. Nothing was in reverse – not the snow, not them – everything was as it was meant to be.

She pushed him away and pulled down her sweater sleeves over her hands. She folded her arms across her chest.

He looked at her once more. Took her in. She was different. The space between places had collapsed, people were propelled through the sky in pressurised cabins, but she was opening up another world in the world.

He got in the taxi and closed the door. She waved once and walked back into the hotel. The Algerian gave him a warm greeting and he returned pleasantries, enough to warm the cab.

The local train stations were all snowed in so they had to drive for an hour to a larger town that was on the main line. At one point in the journey they came up a steep hill and the car slid across the road into a ditch. He got out and pushed. It gave easily. He followed the car up the hill. When he was at the top, the car ahead of him, the brake lights, the exhaust, he found himself at the edge of a cliff and saw the Atlantic breaking on the rocks below.

A few kilometres further on, his mobile rang.

'It's me, it's Danny,' she said. 'I just wanted to say I miss you already.'

'Let me turn around.'

He would have done. She did not reply immediately. He could hear the wind. Then her voice was clearer. She must have cupped her hand over the mouthpiece. 'I'm going for my swim now. Merry Christmas.'

'Merry Christmas, Danny.'

In the last scene of August Strindberg's novella *By the Open Sea*, an arrogant and maniacal fishing inspector, Axel Borg, breaks down when confronted with his own mediocrity, something he has despised in almost everyone else.

A steamer is wrecked on Huvudskär, the island in the Stockholm archipelago to which he has been posted. It is laying on its side just offshore, its white and black funnel broken and its vermilion bottom shining like a blood-stained, shattered breast. He is feverish, half-mad. He staggers along the treeless shore, slipping on the red gneiss scraped clean of lichen by pack ice, and sees dark figures floating and twisted like worms on hooks among the masts and yards of the steamer.

He wades out into the icy waters, the waves slopping over him, and gathers in armfuls of gaily dressed children:

Some had fair fringes on their foreheads, others dark. Their cheeks were rosy and white, and their large, wide-open blue eyes stared straight up at the black sky and neither moved nor blinked.

They were a consignment of dolls.

There is another world in our world, but we have to live in this one. Jellies we are, washed up on the shore.

He knew he had to keep his wits about him. He had resisted the Stockholm syndrome. He was repelled by the Muslim men around him, who chained and beat him, who called him miisteer watir and yet saw him as unclean – monkey, rat, waste – and would not touch him except in violence and gave him drink and food on a plate and cup which were his alone and considered dirty and not to be touched by anyone else, and they would not endow a smile on him. He spat at them when they were knelt in prayer with their backs turned. They were not worth more than spit to him. He spat at them the way he had masturbated in his jail in Kismayo, to invigorate and separate himself from them. It was all the sordid means he had available.

Their minds were weak. They misrepresented their religion. The jihad had trammelled them. They lied to others and to themselves. They had no strategy. Their choice was to fight on and kill more innocents or be annihilated. It was obvious they would choose oblivion over surrender. There was an emptiness in their expressions, which came from not entertaining any doubts. Some of the Somali boys had already died to the world the way Saif had. They were like the bleached and opened badlands. Not dead, not alive. Scarred. They recorded their martyrdom videos outside the shepherd's hut, with the cypress tree in the background.

They were copying the Heaven's Gate cult in America, the first group to document suicides with video testimony. Its members found a collective determination to take their own lives having visited a funfair earlier in the day. They made their video testimony and jumped the earth to a shooting star, so they believed, while their bodies remained on the bunks in California; the bodies, flesh, hair, the mint $5 bill they each had folded in their pocket, their brand new running shoes. They died in shifts, assisting each other. The last members had no one to clean up the vomit from the phenobarbital and vodka they drank, or to remove the plastic bags from their heads which suffocated them.

He stopped. Maybe he had the same dullness in him, maybe he had fallen in a crack. His stories always circled back to death rites. The tap of an axe on a boy's spine.

They drove for a day without stopping and the lorry set them down in a village on the coast south of Kismayo. He was shackled to the wooden railing of a shark-fishing dhow. They sailed south through a night and into the day. The wind was against them. The sea was rough. The fishermen moved barefoot on the dhow, adjusting and readjusting the lateen sail. He was sure they were sailing south to the al-Qaeda training camps in the mangrove swamps around Ras Kamboni, on the border with Kenya.

His shackles had enough play for him to lean out over the water and catch the sea spray. He could also move out of the sun, but it was not possible to stop himself from being rubbed raw. They were far enough from the land for him to wonder at the depth of the water. His guards brought him a bucket to wash himself and looked away when he performed (there was no other word) his toilet.

The boat listed under its unseemly cargo. There were more men at arms now, and the shark men, there were goats, nets and hooks, a brazier on which fish were cooked, and a basket of rice, bananas and mangoes. The arms in the hold were covered with the bodies of black fin sharks and lemon sharks.

'But, as they went farther,' Thomas More continues, in *Utopia*, 'a new scene opened, all things grew milder, the air less burning, the soil more verdant, and even the beasts were less wild.'

135

The dhow had no motor. There was just the slop of the Indian Ocean as it gave, and the stink of the sharks and the shark oil used to caulk the hull. The fishermen had been at sea for a month. They had smoked the shark and marlins over fires on uninhabited islands, where they also made lime from the coral, burning it to such a temperature that it burst when they poured sea water on it.

The next night his shitting was endless. They gave him a can of Fanta. The heavens were hidden behind the clouds. They aimed the dhow out to sea to avoid the reefs and the shallows that would ground a boat in the finest mud. It began to howl. Rain swept in. He slid about on the deck and banged against the sides. Saif and the others were curled up like insects about to die, all armoured and repentant. He heard their prayers issuing forth and could not help but think of the disciples on the Sea of Galilee in a storm. There was only one last living shark aboard, slapping its tail against the deck. The coast lay far away in the night, hot, unlit, as the badlands had been unlit. It was not the winter grey of the French coast, it was another coast entirely; which for centuries a mongrel mix of shark men, traders and clerics had sailed up and down. The Bajunis, keeping close to their unknown islands, the Somalis, the Swahili peoples from as far south as Mozambique, the Comorians, Malagasy, Portuguese and Omanis, the Chinese fleet, the Yemenis, Persians, Gujaratis and Malays.

The pirate Edward England captured treasure from a pilgrim ship sailing to Jeddah and buried it on the Somali coast. England had dug a hole in a dry ravine and laid the treasure chest under a rock there. It was never found. The captain's crew mutinied and put him ashore on a desert island off Madagascar, on account of his uncommon sense of mercy (for a pirate), and England circled there, searching for water and something to eat. His thinking must have been much more depressed than that of a conman beaten and left in a ditch outside Verona, who, with a ducat stitched in his dress, dusted himself down and walked back over the Alps to Munich in the spring sunshine.

136

He looked across the raging sea. Somewhere was the gold and jewels meant for Mecca, unopened, without glitter. Oh, the scale of things was planetary for him then, Somalia was mighty, yet just a piece of the main, the sea larger still; the ocean sank away under him.

James cradled his drink, sipped it like life. Fanta, fanta, fantasy, fantastic, it was orange nectar, a bubbling drink of New Atlantis, and though he was in mortal peril, or because he was, he had a rising sense of excitement, as if buoyed into the *Arabian Nights*, and it comforted him to place the seasick holy warriors of al-Qaeda not a clash of civilisations, but a bunch of brigands who would get what was coming to them.

Professor Danielle Flinders, biomathematics, self-organisation, was what it said on her official Imperial College webpage. She was one of the world's leading researchers on population dynamics of microbial life in the oceans. The microscopic was phantom and massive to her and her lectures were popular because they ranged widely beyond maths to take in biology, physics, geology; even philosophy and literature.

She had written him a letter in which she very seriously claimed that an understanding of microbial life in the deep was necessary for human survival on the planet:

Without that knowledge, we will not be able to comprehend the scale of life on earth, or its ability to regenerate. The fact that life can exist in the darkness, on chemicals, changes our understanding about life everywhere else in the universe.

She was a senior scientist, not the chief scientist. That was perfect. She had responsibility for her work, with none of the bureaucratic burdens

137

of the chief scientist, whose job it was to balance the personalities and goals of those who want sediment core samples, those who want sweeping measurement of the water column, and those who are after one particular deep-sea fish. She had been a chief scientist once. It had been a disaster. She had her father's brains, not his easygoing charm. She was brittle. She excelled, but suffered no fools. That was one problem. The other had been with politically correct individuals. She was black to them, carrying the burden of black history, the meagreness of black science, and they could not bear to criticise her openly. That had led to miscommunication, passive-aggressive behaviour, and recriminations when the expedition failed. It was easier with the French. They appreciated her fluency. They perceived her coolness as elegance and warmed to the intensity she brought to her work.

She kept fit in London, and more so at sea. When it was said she punched her way through a science cruise, it was only the punishment she delivered to the punch-bag in the boat's gym. She built up her cardiovascular strength. When her work was finished she had in the past fallen in with a scientist or a deckhand. Whatever the stolen pleasures of the bunk, she would end the arrangement directly when the ship returned to port.

Though the Fanta was warm and he was chained like a dog and the sharks in the hold were buried in salt, there was something alive and enormous in being set sail on the ocean, something about the flight of the dhow in the wind and no other force, and the smoothness of the deck, where shoes were forbidden, and the planking had been polished by bare feet over a long time.

To set sail was another of the smaller truths. There was landlessness, rocking. The harpooner's cry of *thar she blows!* was another way of saying there she breathes. He lived in a time when no ships sailed the line, when there was no sail cloth, no rope, no horses or carts in the ports, while aboard the supertankers were freezers the size of an admiral's state rooms, filled with meats and fruits; metal cupboards with cartons of treated milk wrapped in plastic, which were a long way advanced from the crates of spring water, wines, almonds, lemons, dry bread and all manner of sauces for salted meat in the stores of eighteenth-century vessels.

The storm abated. The prayers and mutterings continued. There was the rhythmic dousing of barnacles encrusted on the hull and a noise of the planking giving under the weight of the water.

Then it was day, the sun struck the sea. He watched the seabirds touch the crest of the swells, always on the wing. He saw a whale shark big enough to swallow a Jonah, hoovering the life that was invisible to the naked eye. There were gold markings on its back, which the fishermen believed were coins sprinkled by Allah as a reward to the fish for being toothless and having no appetite for meat.

A recent top secret United States Army report predicts mass death for Africans in the coming years. The report's main points will be leaked to the press, and placed alongside the headline points of other similarly depressing reports made by diplomats, spies and political scientists; including those which speak of death by famine, new epidemics, climate change, infestations of insects, methane gas bubbles, or even by meteors. In this context it is a relief to read again the writings of the Russian anarchist Prince Pyotr Kropotkin.

As a child, Pyotr served in the Corps of Pages in St Petersburg; his father owned a thousand souls on the family estate. Pyotr escaped a life in court by enlisting in a Cossack regiment in the wild Amur

139

region of Siberia. Later, as an anarchist in exile, he sought to use a study of the animal kingdom to resolve the two great movements of his day: the liberty of the individual, and the cooperation of the community. Darwin's survival of the fittest theory was brilliant, Kropotkin said, but it did not explain everything. Revolution required other considerations.

Kropotkin believed in the pre-human origin of moral instincts, a mutual aid that draws us together:

> Whenever I saw animal life in abundance, as, for instance, on the lakes where scores of species and millions of individuals came together to rear their progeny; in the colonies of rodents; in the migrations of birds which took place at that time on a truly American scale along the Usuri; and especially in a migration of fallow-deer which I witnessed on the Amur, and during which scores of thousands of these intelligent animals came together from an immense territory, flying before the coming deep snow, in order to cross the Amur where it is narrowest, in all these scenes of animal which passed before my eyes, I saw mutual aid and mutual support carried on to an extent which made me suspect in it a feature of the greatest importance for the maintenance of life, the preservation of each species, and its further evolution.

In other words, the unsociable species is doomed. Kropotkin's example of the deer crossing the Amur still intrigues. How did the deer understand their common cause was to cross the Amur River in greatest numbers at its narrowest point? How many of them were swept away in discovering the narrowest point? Did the birds give the deer a clue? When the deer found the narrowest point how did they agree upon it? Were there deer who refused to support the decision? Dissenters? Mutual aid extends to man. In exile, Kropotkin interviewed a Kentish boatman who risked his life to save some drowning souls. What had made him row out into the storm?

'I don't rightly know myself,' said the boatman to the prince, 'I saw men clinging to the mast, I heard their cries, and all at once I thought: I must go!'

There are other examples, as of the old man in Karelia who dug his grave in the summer as a service to his village in the winter, when the earth was frozen hard. Or the mutual aid practised by the crews of the Hansa trading ships on the Baltic and the North Sea who, if they were caught in a storm and believed they would drown, proclaimed each man to be the equal of the other, and all to be at the mercy of God and the waves.

The statue of Christ of the Abyss stands 17 metres underwater in La Spezia harbour. Even at that depth, the world we know recedes. The sun appears to contract and harden like the pupil of an eye when a torch is shone on it. The water is blue. Red is already filtered out from the spectrum; if there is a cut the blood looks black.

Those who strap on aqualungs and dive deeper find something darker. They drift in their wetsuits, calling ground control, flippers barely moving. Already the sea is becoming the ocean. They look down and see a pit. Davy Jones's locker.

Do not think to swim below. The ocean is already pushing into ears, sinuses, temples, the softness of eyes and the harpsichord strings behind the kneecaps.

They brought him rice and marlin. He drank copious amounts of rainwater. He was burned by the sun. He told himself he would remain upstanding, but he was doubled over. He was an Englishman without

141

shade. He was held by enemies whose lives he could not grasp, the kind of characters who appear in cartoons with no back story; heavily armed and claiming a significance of history he could not decipher.

He managed to arrange a cloth over his face. He closed his eyes and saw the feet of a swan in an icy pond, from below, pushing away the slush; white swans in the boreal, black swans in the austral. He saw himself diving down into his swimming pool in Nairobi, then coming up for air. In his delirium, he sailed himself into the harbour of a flat island in the north, the shape of which appeared cut out with a scallop shell. It was a windswept island with only a few trees; pale, with tussock grass, heather, and a single dark hill rising up in the distance from another island in the group. The stone quay in the harbour was strewn with the creels and the orange plastic fish boxes commonly found in the fishing harbours of north England and Scotland, and there was at the end of the quay a narrow department store built from local sandstone – a flatiron building – whose opulent and glowing window displays contrasted with the inclement and solitary nature of this New Atlantis.

Torpidity reigned. The dhow cut slowly through the water. They were coming to Ras Kamboni: Kenya was a short sail away. How quickly he could make it on a speedboat from there to Lamu. He might shower that evening as a free man at the Peponi Hotel and take supper on the veranda overlooking the sea. Crab and mango salad and chilled wine. But that was a fantasy.

They came around a peninsula and grounded the dhow on a crescent beach that was in every respect the opposite of the harbour in New Atlantis.

The Italians called the village Chiamboni, the British called it Dick's Head. Some of its buildings were low with tin roofs that flashed in the sunlight, others were tall like the houses of Lamu, with flat roofs shaded by canopies, candy-coloured in the Somali fashion. He was untied. They pushed a gun into his back and he jumped down and waded in his kikoi through unreadable water to the land.

He was marched and dragged through Chiamboni. He tripped and fell. He laughed. He listened to himself, like a bird to its failing song, curious at where the noise came from. His laugh was more of a cackle. Could it really be him? He felt humiliated.

The alleys of Chiamboni were cramped and piled up with the rubble of collapsed houses. An open sewer dribbled milky water, fetid with lumps of dung. There were elaborate doorways in the Swahili style, and others with just a piece of cloth, and families teemed in single rooms, quieting as they went by, just as the boys playing table football in the street in Kismayo had hushed, and all of this repeating, labyrinthine, until they came out onto the sand to a remarkable Italian colonial building at the edge of the village. It was set directly before the dunes, like a house in a children's story.

The *Pourquoi Pas?* pitched in heavy seas on her first night out from Iceland. Danny lay in her bunk listening to Bruckner's Fifth Symphony on high-fidelity headphones. There was a light over her head at the end of the bunk. The sheets were white and crisp: she always brought her own.

The cabin smelled of diesel. She became drowsy. She took Bruckner in and contemplated the Greenland Sea as an orchestra pit and the entire Los Angeles Philharmonic dropping into it. The sound changed and carried underwater like whale song.

The house was built on the model of a plan by Enrico Prampolini, the Futurist whose mural decorated the post office in La Spezia. It was an indulgence of a colonial officer from Turin, who wanted to leave

143

a mark at the southernmost point of the Italian Empire. When the house was built it must have been possible to take a cocktail and sit on a deckchair and look out over the Indian Ocean. There was an inscription in the entrance hall and surviving parts of a clock. Everything else was gone, except the quality of the building itself; its unwrinkled concrete, the steps up on all sides, the immense fireplace used one day a year, the stencils of organisms on the plasterwork and the flagstones arranged in harlequin patterns characteristic of Prampolini's polychromatism. It was airy, with sand over the patterned floors. There were goats and sheep in the courtyard. The overflow of the latrine was easily mistakable at first sight for yellow mud. The men slept together in one room. The roof was for the women and children.

He was led into a room in which Yusuf the Afghan was on his knees in prayer. When the prayers were done Yusuf looked up and clapped his hands and went to each of his fighters and kissed their heads and hands. James stood between Saif and Qasab; Yusuf did not acknowledge him. He was marched into an adjoining room, the original dining room, which was filled with new recruits. It was the usual scene; weapons, ammunition boxes used as seats as in the mosque in Kismayo, food in the centre; king fish, spaghetti. There was a television and a video recorder hooked up to a car battery. Yusuf was opposed to public entertainment. Television was banned, so was popular music. The al-Qaeda camps in Afghanistan had shown Hollywood action films – John Rambo fighting with the holy warriors in Afghanistan against the strutting Soviets – but those days were over. Instead there were discs of their own manufacture showing beheadings and suicide-bombings in Somalia and Iraq. Yusuf made an exception for classic Disney; he loved *Snow White*, *Dumbo* and the rest. His personal favourite was *Bambi*.

It was crowded; it felt like a school to him. The new recruits were very young and the others behaved like older pupils, telling them to be quiet, cuffing them. He wondered which of them would volunteer to be a suicide bomber. What would they say to make sense of self-destruction? (He had wanted to ask these questions of Saif, but the moment had not presented itself.)

The mood was excited. Even Qasab smiled and leaned in when Yusuf had *Bambi* turned on. They stopped the film at one of the songs. James's hands were untied and his wrists were daubed with ointment where the rope had cut into them. He was given a pen and paper and asked to write down the words. They replayed it several times. He wrote them down and passed the paper along:

> I bring you a song
> And I sing as I go
> For I want you to know
> That I'm looking for romance
> I bring you a song
> In the hope that you'll see
> When you're looking at me
> That I'm looking for love!

The film was paused again near the end, at a scene where the forest was burning and Bambi fell in the flames and was bucked to his feet by his father, the great prince stag. He transcribed:

'It is man. He is here again. There are many this time. We must go deep into the forest. Hurry, follow me!'

Yusuf stood up in front of a stilled image of rising flames and urged them to identify with Bambi. The Crusaders were man. The forest was the mangrove in which the believers were safe. It did not trouble Yusuf that they were watching an American narrative. To him, it was pure. It had religious worth.

James glanced around the room. The fighters were spellbound. There was something more to it. When he understood, it was obvious. The faces were bathed in Disney colours: the same pinks, blues and greens which dominated in portraits of jihadists; with songbirds fluttering around turbans, an armful of flowers, gun on lap, and always in the background a forest with a cornflower-blue sky and a yellow sun that itself had been lifted from *Bambi* in the form of Chinese computer wallpaper. It was the art as much as the story that held them. The Crusaders were burning the Islamic state and Bambi was the innocent combatant, as they were represented in the martyrdom videos.

The windows were open. The mosquitoes were just out there in the wind. Music carried from the village. It drove Qasab into a rage. He sent two boys to put a stop to it. One wore a grenade in his belt. There was screaming, wailing. After a few minutes, the two came back with a smashed radio.

There was the braying of a wounded donkey, the shuffling around him, the oiling of guns, then not even that; only the surf booming on the reef.

The men of Chiamboni were trap fishing for yellow tuna under the full moon. They waded and swam out with nets and spears. The women were on the beach collecting cowries, which were sold to Kenyan traders, who in turn employed beach boys to sell the shells to tourists up and down the Kenyan coast.

Somali beaches were the finest in Africa, and this one was very wild, very beautiful, bone white, and backed by the east-facing dunes. The stars were all in their ocean station, the turtles laying eggs, there were large-toothed fish in the shallows and mangroves holding the dry land together. There was surf and in other places the water was unmoving, warm as blood, and full of life. He imagined the dotted scuttle of jade crabs to their burrows. How many crabs was that? How many separate journeys? He saw a heap of shell fragments and bones, a midden that amounted to 10,000 years of human leavings.

*

The south wind blew. It lifted scarves from the floor. It scattered paper and turned pages in an open prayer book. Dust kicked up from the alleys in the village. Sewage dribbled from buildings to beach, not milky any more but green with weed and reactions. It wetted a mahogany boat that was lain on its side.

He remembered something from his childhood, of how the ancient Britons worshipped the south wind and divided the elements into flowers, fire, sky, soil, mist and freshwater, but were confounded by saltwater.

He thought of many other things besides, more personal things. Of course he did.

He was consumed with the desire to escape. He was to be taken the next day to a camp hidden in the mangrove. That was to enter a place of martyrs. He was only Mr Water to them, a curiosity, yet he knew too much. They would watch for him. Bribe? Firefight? He had to try. But there were fighters sleeping on either side of the door, there were guards downstairs, the night was lunar-lit, and he was so weak, standing was difficult for him, he needed medical attention, and, besides, he was tied hand to foot and only by chance had he the Futurist window view.

Two skiffs had appeared on the bay in the morning. He was thrown into one of them. Maize meal and spaghetti were loaded along with dried mangoes and papayas, tinned fish, turtle meat, medicines, mosquito netting, candles, kerosene, fuel, knives, guns, ammunition and explosives: even the smallest jihad needed its provisions. The scene was Somali – the fighters jostling, the scarves, the teeth, fringed by seas and swamps and backed by furnace scrub – yet in the breaking light the skiffs stood in contrast to the darker sky, and it rained, silver, everywhere. It was high tide, and when they sped off the bay and Chiamboni looked like the gunmetal Thames, and London at Michaelmas. Captivity was a humiliation, it was also a loneliness that made you want to see something else in front of you. They steered into a lagoon

147

and the tropical heat buffeted him. They opened the throttle on the Yamaha outboards (bought or stolen from Captain Andy's Marine Supplies in Mombasa) and chattered over the water like skis on ice; thence into tidal channels, a creek, another, towards the camp hidden in the swamp. It became steadily more tenebrous and overhanging. The outboards were lifted up and the men poled the boats forward. At some points the fighters jumped off and pushed the skiffs over a sandbar into a cut of water. The mangrove roots were underwater at high tide and exposed at low tide. They were tubular, lifelike. They looked like hands of puppets held in horror. Just like in the wadi, there was concern about the Americans. They sought to keep themselves out of sight under the branches. Uncle Sam knew nothing, Uncle Sam saw everything.

Down narrower creeks like capillaries, to a shallow island which had a crossing point for elephants from the mainland. The camp was where the moat stood a little deeper. It had survived the Ethiopian and American strafing and bombing, but had been abandoned and occupied by Boni hunter-gatherers, at the northern edge of their range.

Several Boni men stood before them. James's first impression was not of a paradisal people, but of children gone feral.

They laughed when Saif interrogated them about the fishing.

'We don't fish!' said one, in Swahili. 'We are Boni! We hunt!'

They had dug pits in the sandy soil. Animals fell in and the Boni speared them.

'There is space for you here,' another said. 'There are dik-dik. There are pigs.'

'Pigs!' Saif shouted. 'What does he take us for?'

If the ancient hunter-gatherer Boni are known at all it is for the version of Kropotkin's mutual aid they practise with a bird they call mirsi.

They whistle to mirsi and mirsi whistles back. It leads the Boni to the wild honey in the trees in the bush. The Boni shin up the trees and smoke out the hives, taking the honey and honeycombs, being sure to leave the bird a generous share in wax and bee larvae.

The Boni are resistant to bee stings and exhibit little sense of vertigo in the high branches of trees. They are an ancient people, related to the Twa Pygmies of Congo. They go barefoot, their walk is peculiarly solid, from the pelvis, very different from the stride of the Somalis, which comes loosely from the shoulder.

A Boni boy achieves manhood by spearing a buffalo, an elephant, or other big animal. On the night before their first hunt the girls pleasure the boys and smear their heads with coconut oil. If a boy fails the hunting test, he will be denied the right to marry. Brides are expensive and have to be paid for in bush meat, skins, sugar or cash. The kidnapping and the rape of girls by Boni men who cannot afford the marriage portion is common.

She stood at the railings. The air was raw. The *Pourquoi Pas?* was approaching Jan Mayen Island. She wanted to see it. There was salt on her lips and spray on her Icelandic sweater and tangerine-coloured jeans. She wrapped herself in a sleeping bag and sat on a deckchair and opened the *New Scientist*. She furled the magazine tight against the wind and read the latest news on nanotechnology. When she was done, she watched a matinee: fog and sea. Gulls wheeled above cold rich swells. There were pieces of ice and icebergs. There were pilot whales riding the bow wave. It was beautiful to watch them. A killer whale cut loops under migrating geese. It went in and out of the water. It sparkled. She could see from its dorsal fin that it was a male, old and tired. It appeared troubled by the thrumming of the ship. It made her think of the changes that had occurred in the Greenland Sea in its

149

lifetime. When it was birthed there were hardly any ships. There were no submarines. There were no engines, klaxons; no man-made noises. There were many seals and fish then, whereas now there was such a competition the killer whale was forced to trail geese in the hope that one might fall from the sky.

The ocean was being fished out, poisoned and suffering acidification. Quite apart from the vessels there were sonar arrays and other electronics that ruptured the orientation of sea mammals. And if sea mammals could become so disorientated as to beach themselves, so could man exterminate himself. Man had hardly taken breath from the Stone Age and yet was altering the flow of rivers, cutting up hills and discarding the materials that would be easily identifiable to future geologists. The anthropocene: a geological age marked by plastic.

There was not enough funding for ocean research. If the financial crisis continued, there would be even less money available: the Greenland Sea expedition was her best chance to gather data for years to come. There was a faulty sense of perspective, she thought. The looking up, the looking out. Through difficulty to the stars, never to the deep. The worry for the skin, not the lungs. The ocean was too immediate, too familiar. You did not need a launch pad, you could just drop into it: it could wait.

Yet there could be no serious work on climate change without understanding marine living systems. The change was real, she was certain of that. The water under the ship, carried through the Fram Strait on the East Greenland Current, had warmed by 1.9 degrees Celsius since 1910. That was 1.4 degrees Celsius more than the increase during the tenth- to thirteenth-century Medieval Warm Period.

She was doing her part. She had been a proponent and a player in the Census for Marine Life and the Deep Water Chemosynthetic Ecosystems. She was an adviser in Southampton, at IFREMER and at the Deep Submergence Facility in Woods Hole. She believed manned submersibles were vital. They provided the necessary leap of imagination, the human connection to the deep. Machines could complement them. Hundreds of drones could fly far under the sea, quietly, at all hours, providing a constant flow of information to the surface.

Then there was the biological revolution. It was possible to see creatures that had never been noticed before, the living matter of the minestrone, of which only one recently discovered species of pico-phytoplankton in the upper layers of the ocean was reckoned to have a biomass equivalent to the insect life in the Congo River basin. The diversity was overwhelming. She was interested in numbers, in percola-tion, but almost by accident she had discovered new species. She had overseen the mapping of their DNA, given them a genetic barcode and put them in the book of life (others said the hard drive of life). One of the papers she co-authored with Thumbs had incidentally reinforced the view of some biologists that there were microbes in the sea that were deliberately rare. These microbes were waiting for condi-tions to change so they could become abundant. She found this a very powerful thought. It changed her idea of what a lifespan meant. A microbe waiting a million years, holding to a different rhythm through those many sunrises and sunsets. What was that rhythm?

The *Pourquoi Pas?* rolled and the portholes were washed with seawater. It rolled back and she saw how the glass shone the length of the ship. The fog closed in. She sang to herself:

> In South Australia, my native land
> Full of rocks and thieves and sand
> I wish I was on Australia's strand
> With a bottle of whisky in my hand.

It was a shanty her father liked to sing. If the world forgot its sea shanties, forgot the sea, it would be even harder to speak of the strange-ness of what was under the waves.

151

They passed through the fog bank and Jan Mayen appeared then with the clarity of a photograph taken with the highest quality camera; thin beaches, blues and greys of augite and pyroxene. The volcano looked like Mount Fuji, only more spectral. The cone coughed up cinders. The fire inside of it glimmered on the underside of the clouds. The iron ore on the slopes, the snowfields and shreds of mist about the rim were the sulphurous way in. Looking at it, considering how it plunged into the sea to a point where it swarmed with seismic tremors and was suppurated with magma, she felt she understood what Saint Brendan said when he had seen the volcano on his incredible sixth-century voyage: that this way into hell, the opening to the infernal regions every damned soul must take.

She pulled a notepad from her bag and a felt-tip pen. She began to write James a letter. It felt good to write to him. These big thoughts were like blackened icebergs. Even in her, with her commitment, they were too big to hold onto. Yet the more she worked on them the less desperate she felt. They effected in her an almost religious sentiment. It was not submission – she would work – it was a Buddhist sense of resignation and a feeling of responsibility to her own living form. To Danny Flinders. The very precariousness of her condition and more generally the condition of mankind made her body and choices more precious to herself. It was incumbent upon her to live fully; to give and to receive. The thought of him someplace in Africa brought out a tenderness in her. What she wrote to him then was very intimate, deliberately containing small things which are quickly forgotten: she had a cold, she had managed to avoid having a cabin-mate, Thumbs was in a sweat because he was missing a rock festival and the livestreaming was not working, there were bird droppings on her sleeping bag. It felt good to write with pen on paper in such a place, in such a mood. It felt permanent.

The colours turned pale. It was gelid. Her breath was like steam. Heroic friendships were being formed below decks, the *Nautile* was

152

being equipped in the aft hangar for its dive the next day, but she was content to remain up above a little longer, wrapped up, staring out at the productive waters, the shearwaters, storm petrels and eider ducks.

If you talk about the acceleration that is in the world, you have to talk about the advances in computational power. There was a recent momentous day when a computer at the Los Alamos National Laboratory in New Mexico achieved petaflop speed. One thousand trillion calculations a second. How to conceive of such a rate? If everyone in the world were given a pocket calculator and ordered to tap out sums for six hours a day, it would take them until the twenty-fourth century to match the calculations a petaflop computer can perform in a day.

The exaflop is the next step in the history of computing: one quintillion calculations a second. Then the zettaflop, yottaflop and the xeraflop. The goal is nothing less than to slow down time and colonise it. Of course, a petaflop computer uses more electricity than the power grid of an African city. Then there is the problem of asking useful questions of it.

The sand around the camp was filled with thorns. There were long acacia thorns and round thorns spiked like depth charges. Even with flip-flops, his feet were punctured at every step.

One of the Boni laid a British Enfield rifle and a Soviet PPS sub-machine gun on the ground together with a few bullets and strips of dried meat. The Boni beckoned one of his children forward. She could not eat. Her belly was swollen and her skin festered with sores around the ankles and the calves. When the man appealed for help, Saif had him beaten with sticks. A leg cracked under a blow and the beating stopped. It was strange: Saif wanted to see a jinn, but he refused to look the Boni in the eye.

'You are not good Muslims,' Saif told them. 'You worship trees. You eat pigs. You are not welcome on our island. You must go.'

The Boni were expressionless. There was no fear, anger, or bitterness apparent in their faces, just the resignation of the enslaved. They left quickly with the injured hunter and their few possessions: bows and arrows, spears, pots and palm matting. One woman gathered a bundle of clothing and strapped it to her back, while the younger women carried the children. The jihadists gave them kerosene and sugar.

James spoke out in favour of the Boni and was punched in the face. Perhaps it was because he was a witness to the unkindness, or perhaps it was the way he stared so rudely at the wine-coloured callus on the forehead of one of the Pakistanis, where the young man struck his forehead to the ground in prayer. Perhaps it was just because morale was low.

It was not true that the jihadists were self-sufficient and needed nothing more than a prayer mat. They had had high hopes of this camp where there had been so many martyrs before them. They had expected more. The boys from Mogadishu were especially desolate. They had seen a documentary in a video shack about the British Army and had persuaded themselves that the jihad had these facilities. Instead of a shower block and a canteen there were only ruined huts, the roofs collapsed, with the water a walk through the overgrown bush.

There was a baobab tree in the centre of the camp that afforded shade and shelter from the rain. He was ordered to make his own shelter under the tree. He took mangrove stems and drove them into the sand and hung up the mosquito net. He made a palm roof and scooped out a hollow in the sand. He was bound again inside the netting, but with such a length of rope that he could crawl freely and see the comings and goings of the camp.

154

The first days were spent repairing the huts, hacking out routes in the bush, collecting firewood, and digging latrines. It was hard. They sandbagged the main hut with food aid sacks filled with wet sand. On each of the sacks was a Stars and Stripes and the words *Gift of the People of the United States.*

A fighter fell into a Boni trap and was sent back to Chiamboni with a broken thighbone. There was an infestation of flies, also scorpions. They slept outside on plastic sheeting, under mosquito nets. Food was in short supply. They had handfuls of maize meal, fish and crab. Spaghetti was rationed.

They pinned up a picture of Osama bin Laden. His body was drowned, yet remained living to them. They played games on a laptop, including one where you got to fight Christians in the sixth-century Holy Land. They trained with rocket-propelled grenades and explosives. They trained with knives. There was no mobile-phone signal; the only connection with the world was by speedboat.

Days passed. Weeks. Baboons encircled the camp. The females had red arses to compare with the blue testes of the male colobus monkeys. He watched the baboons coming and going, quarrelling over fruit and scraps. He studied their personalities. He named them after his captors. They were dog-human; they pissed like dogs, but their faces were human.

It was the French polar explorer Jean-Baptiste Charcot, who, on his many voyages to the Greenland Sea,* discovered that the

---

* *Charcot's boat, the original* Pourquoi Pas?*, sank off the coast of Iceland in 1936, drowning him together with many of his crew.*

temperature of the Hadal deep is a uniform four degrees Celsius around the world. Its sole virtue is constancy. Its processes are uniform. Cold water percolates into the rock, is superheated, and spurts from the chimneys of hydrothermal vents. It dissolves minerals and metals in the rock and, in this way, provides the ingredients for chemical life in what would otherwise be a deathly night, visited only by matter from above.

Until the discovery of hydrothermal vents off the Galapagos Islands in 1977, scientists assumed that life on earth was photosynthetic and belonged to the surface. It was the other way around: photosynthetic life came later, when cells strayed to the top where they were cooked for millions of years before evolving a way to absorb the light, and all the while the chemosynthetic life in the abyss was evolving a stability we cannot hope for.

The hydrothermal vents are only a small part of it. In the fissures, crevices, clefts and cracks; in the volcanic pus, in all the amazing lattices of the deep, are heat-loving or hyperthermophile protists, archaea, fungi and especially bacteria, which together constitute the earliest life on our planet. They are chemosynthetic, with no need of the sun. They live off hydrogen, carbon dioxide or iron. They excrete methane, or eat it. Some breathe in rust to produce magnetic iron. They feed on the anaerobic and on what is no longer living. When you place them in a Petri dish, they multiply into a colony visible to the naked eye. If you dwell on them they change the way we see ourselves. They are the factory workers, unquestioning, dynamic: the base. Less than one per cent of them have been identified, they are a part of you. You carry a weight of them in your belly and on your skin.

The microbial life of the deep exists in the queerest plane, where worms live in scalding pools and keep fleeces of microbes on their backs that are even more extraordinary than those that live on the timbers of our eyelashes.

156

In the white night of the fourth day out of Iceland, the *Pourquoi Pas?* dropped anchor over the underworld they sought. Enki was the northernmost hydrothermal vent field yet discovered, with some of the largest recorded sulphide deposits. The water that poured from its chimneys was 399 degrees Celsius. There was proof of a chemosynthetic life cycle, with acid-feeding bacteria at its foundation, working up to tube worms, white clams, and other bivalves. It was extraordinarily large and ancient. More than that was unclear. The 2011 expedition had discovered the field near where the Knipovich and Mohn undersea ridges joined after weeks of dragging a CTD (where C was conductivity, T was temperature and D was depth) sensor behind the boat in sawtooth patterns. The sensor looked for anomalies. When it found them, it took a sample of vent water, which could then be analysed for telltale levels of dissolved hydrogen and methane oxidised in the water column by microorganisms. Her challenge for 2012 was to scrape from a fissure some richer material, of mathematical consequence.

The first scheduled dives to Enki were for orientation and mapping. The next were for the geologists. The dives for the biologists and mathematicians were to take place close to the end of the cruise. There were various teams of biologists. The evolutionary group were working towards extracting DNA. Another was looking at viruses; they wanted to know how they in their sickness spread from one vent field to another. The French and Swiss astrobiologists Danny and Thumbs were working closely with were gathering samples on behalf of the European Space Agency. The hope was to identify new microorganisms. Claude, the French leader of their team, had placed a bet that life would be found in the methane oceans of Titan in his lifetime. He felt that the search for extraterrestial life was compromised by surface chauvinism:

157

it looked only on the outside of planets, moons and rocks, not deep in the cracks where it was more likely to be. She agreed. Man's fixation with façades, with outward appearances, was another reason why there was not more interest in oceanography.

She took a bullish view. Microbial life was tenacious. It swarmed even in mineshafts and caves. Seen from up close, the cracks in the sea floor were like the cross-hatching on a metal-plate engraving. She believed that some of them went down 8 kilometres into the mantle, and were carpeted with a density of microbial life that, taken together with the deep biota, was more than all the photosynthetic life on the surface of the planet combined. To prove her thesis she had to come up with methods of counting the methanogens, the hyperthermophilic autotrophic iron reducers, and the peculiar states and leagues of archaea and bacteria. She had also tried to identify the boundary which separated the living part from where there was no life and to understand the percolation between existence and non-existence.

What they were doing at sea was the start. Once she and Thumbs were back in London, they would assemble the data and send problems – mathematical complexity, the levels of hierarchy which bridged a microbe to the ecosystem – to teams of biomathematicians in Spain and America.

The *Nautile* was prepared at night. It dived in the morning. A bell was rung on the boat in the afternoon, when it was on its way back to the surface. People went out onto the deck. They guessed on where the pregnancy in the waters would be. The *Nautile* looked both small and dramatic from a distance. White and blue, a piece of china. Frogmen sped out on ribbed inflatables to it. They dived in and secured it so that it could be towed back. When the checks were done, the crew of three emerged weary and triumphant through the hatch. Their initial success was less a scientific one than a human one; they had returned. There was often an expression of wonderment. Some of the scientists shook their heads: they had ascended like Orpheus from the soup which contained the magnitude of species, and which would be the sanctuary of life on earth for as long as it kept spinning, primitive, consistent, constant, offering protection from solar flares, nuclear radiation, comets and other yet unknown human crimes.

An Ogadeni knelt on the other side of the netting, poking him with a stick like a zoo animal and watching him intently. He glared back. He saw the desert in the man's eyes. They were the kidney-damaged pair of a camel herder, not pellucid and darting, but cloudy, rheumy and bloodshot from years of drinking muddy water, camel milk and urine.

He turned over. He could not sleep for more than an hour at a time. Sometimes the sky revolved. He was nauseous. He was forever crawling out of the shadow of the baobab. He thought it was falling on him.

They had been there for months by then. The days had run together. The rot in his netting was making him sick and there was such a heat and outside there were the moving dots of mosquitoes whining at night. He could find no resolution to his anger. He was losing resolve, losing his sense of himself, of his story. His capacity for solving problems was diminishing. He was unloved.

He really was a dog. He was ordered out each day for his meal. Depending on the mood of the fighters he was helped across the encampment or hit and shouted at. He had learned to identify body language and when any of them approached him quickly he curled himself up for protection. During one kicking a line from a song repeated:

Like some cat from Japan.

She held an open house in the lab one evening. Thumbs selected the vinyl records and placed them on his turntable; classic rock, then funk. She ground the coffee beans.

Colleagues wandered in and traded freshly baked pastries for cups of coffee. The conversation was mostly about music, to begin with. There was no discussion of politics; scientists seem to exist slightly out of time in that way. When the alcohol came out there was a general commentary about microbial metabolism, the hydrogen shitters, and what that might mean for a new generation of fuel cells and the grail of clean energy. There was talk of the abyss itself, its carbon sinks of salp, and whether pollution could be taken from the air and injected into it. It often came back to climate change, because there was research money available for it, and tenure for any bright young academic who could make of the vasty deep an engine or rubbish bin. To the backing of funk, another turn in the conversation concerned vertical transport in the global ocean, VERTIGO. Specifically, how to track ocean currents using elements like thorium, which stuck to marine snow and decayed at a stable rate.

Then Thumbs held the floor.

'Put yourself in the future,' he said. 'Out in space. You're property developers. You've found a planet a decent distance from a sun. You buy the place. Now you have to animate it. You put in air, water and microbial life. How to give it a lived-in look? You need to get back to the basics; dig in ponds, marshes; turf the hills, plant oaks, lay out groves, vineyards; introduce deer and foxes.

'What kind of house would we build?'

Thumbs raised his hand and gulped down some liquor. 'Roman, definitely. A villa of the kind found in third-century England; mosaic floors, baths, fireplaces. You'd have space-age fittings too, of course, land sloping down to a stream, and stables filled with horses.'

160

'No cars?'

'No. This would be marketed as a planet you come to slow down. You arrive out of hyperspace, steady yourself, get your transfusion or whatever, then swap your spacesuit for a toga and ride home along a cobbled Roman road through woods and across fields under twin moons. The autumn effect, the frost, and the rest of it would just be climate control.'

She was very happy in evenings like this one, when science seemed a shared enterprise, not a jigsaw of vanities. Thumbs kept changing the records, slowing them down. When they got to acid jazz they abandoned conversation.

They worked through the night with lab assistants. The *Pourquoi Pas?* had set anchor north of Jan Mayen, directly over the Enki field. It was a stormy night. It rained and sleeted through the midnight sun. They were thrown about, but the instruments and computers were screwed down into the wooden counters and fastened with bungee rope and not a dial moved except of its own accord.

They took turns to prepare the samples gathered by the *Nautile*. The treatment was mechanical. The scrapings were soft, whitish and stank of rotten eggs. The vent fluids were gathered using titanium bottles, which did not corrode. Each bottle had a snorkel and a trigger, which could be released from inside the submersible.

They used a spectrophotometer to test light absorption in the sulphides and a microscope showed up the teeming yellow cities on the glass slides. They did their own quantitative culturing and made use of the microscopy, microprobes and spectroscopies the astrobiologists undertook. It was the embodied end of mathematics.

She finished work at three o'clock. She slept a few hours and then ran and punched in the gym. She had a brunch of toast, pasta and an apple, then went to a meeting with the other senior scientists on the bridge to specify the scientific payload for each dive.

161

She was distracted; there was something like a hair-drier blowing out hot air by the door where she was standing. She kept looking out of the windows at the sea.

When the meeting was over she stayed on the bridge and studied the undersea charts for the Greenland Sea. They were fictitious. The soundings were off. Even with its clumped lines of reversed contours, the charts failed to capture the depth of the ocean, the day spent sinking into it.

Odile is an early novella by the French writer Raymond Queneau. Odile waits for her husband Travy at the docks in Marseilles when he returns from Greece. Travy looks out from the deck of his ship at all the piled-up pieces of the port and sees her at last at the barricade behind the customs shed, among the hustlers and porters.

Living in 1920s France as Travy and Odile lived was harder than chasing your own tail or balancing on a pinhead. People often went to bed hungry. Yet Travy fell properly in love with Odile. The story ended and the boy started to live. Or rather, he started to live again.

The scene at the docks in Marseilles would be very different if Queneau wrote it today. Indeed, he could not write it in the same way. It would be a flight from Athens to Paris. A budget airline, not a proper one. There would be less tension and a diminished sense of arrival. Travy would come out of arrivals at Charles de Gaulle. Ignoring the minicab drivers and the policemen, he would follow the directions she had texted him, and they would embrace at a newsstand beyond.

The mosquito net was the only barrier between James and the monkeys. A colobus grabbed the netting in its small fists and began to tear it. He batted it away and was surprised at its flimsiness, how little it weighed.

He reflected on the violence in his life. Not the violence of his youth, in combat operations, but in his more recent intelligence work. He was like anyone else. He had different faces.

You hit fast and hard. A flurry of punches was best. He had dealt with two Welsh mercenaries who wanted to sell arms to Somali jihadists. One was from a pit village, the other was of Somali extraction. Instead of going through procedures, he found a Ugandan to beat the men and pour sand in their eyes. He tricked them into thinking it was the work of the jihadists.

It was no longer safe to travel to Chiamboni: he was told that Yusuf had gone to Kenya and from there to Tanzania. Water became a problem at the camp. The filters were broken. There was no more iodine. The water from the well was boiled. Still, it was spewed up. They sucked on sweet fruit and drank coconut milk, but could not quench their thirst. The spring water served in metal cups at the shepherd's hut in the badlands was a luxury from a past life. The hope was always for rain. The downpours saved them. The thirstier the fighters were, the more solicitous they became. *How must we store the rainwater? How do we keep it clean?* He told them. When the rain filled their makeshift cisterns, he shouted out until they gagged him. It was pathetic. His anger was ridiculous. But they were so puerile. They had ambitions of dominion, but could not feed themselves. They were like hyenas in an African story who stack themselves up into the sky, one atop the other, because they had been told the moon was a sweetmeat they could reach up and eat.

The gunmetal Thames, the jinn pit, his swimming pool in Muthaiga – then there was Winckler, the French spy he cooperated with, standing there, winking at him. Winckler? There was nothing to remember about the man. They had met in busy bars in Nairobi and other African capitals. Their business was conducted quickly. Winckler always insisted on buying beer in bottles. It was Winckler who had got him smoking again. What else? Winckler wheezed. He had a facial tic that made his eyelids flutter. Yellow bridgework. There was no more. It was like the bony Russians. There was no reason. Winckler swimming, Winckler underwater; fleshy, grey lips, snaggy teeth, an abyssal fish with a lantern shedding bioluminescence where his balding forehead had been.

One time he looked up and saw a passenger jet flying unusually low. It looked like a Yemeni Airways plane. It was probably heading for Sana'a. Just to sense the world moving about him seemed very important. He tried to remember what it was like to be a small child and all the little things his mother had done for him which he had forgotten. Bedtime again, much earlier: feeding him, bathing him, reading to him, laying down next to him until he fell asleep.

He was taken to wash himself in the creek in the evenings. He watched the boys catching crabs on its banks. They were featherweight, yet sank to their hips in smooth mud. They took long hooked sticks and worked them into the crab holes. They pulled quickly when a crab attacked the stick. A single jerk, not allowing the crab to dig itself deeper in. They held the crabs by their back legs. It was one of the only times he saw them laugh, holding the crabs away from them, and watching them snip the air.

He was finally the man with bones made of mists who could find no solid banks. There were flies, a whirring of beetles. He wanted to be done with it and put his head in the water. It was silent. He imagined the fighters in the water. Most of them could not swim. They would go blindly, flailing, not ever barrelling forward, their penises would be small and curled up like seahorses, and water would pour in when they opened their mouths.

*

The embers of a fire were burning low in the dark. He saw mouths moving. One exclaimed, another told it to shut up. There were theological disputes. There were martyrs' tales.

One night he was allowed to sit with the group while Saif told the story of how Sheikh Ahmed Salim Swedan was killed by an American air strike in Pakistan. May the blessings of Allah be upon him.

He smiled. Swedan was a Kenyan who had run a transport business in Mombasa and been recruited into al-Qaeda through a football team run by Usama al-Kini. The team targeted young men from poor families – frustrated because there were no jobs and no money for them to get married.

The aft-hangar was large enough to hold a helicopter. The *Nautile* sat on a cradle inside of it. French rock music blasted out.

It was her turn – she was to dive in the morning – but she hung back and let the crew get on with it. The *Nautile* dived a hundred times a year. The preparations had become routine. The submersible was washed down with freshwater to reduce corrosion, then everything was methodically checked: valves, radios; the computer booted up, the floats attached, finally the science payload in baskets, snorkel bottles, cameras, thermal-imaging devices and the robotic arm which was to stretch out to scrape a sample. When they tested the lights on the craft it was like a UFO landing inside the hangar.

'Professor Flinders? We're ready now.'

She examined the payload. She had her checklist. She went through it. When she was finished she smiled.

'Perfect! Thank you.'

She gifted them some bottles of wine and they went outside the hangar and drank and smoked together. It was a treasure sky just then, streaked with gold. There was a barbecue. They grilled fish that had been caught on the hooked lines hung off the sides of the boat. She ate a salmon steak with salad and a baguette and washed it down with wine. Everyone spoke English. A Norwegian scientist poured out glasses of aquavit. She might have fallen for someone in a moment like that; in the Arctic, so capacious, so soothing. But she felt herself to be half of a whole and was no longer interested.

She was focused: for the hours she was underwater she wanted to be as sharp in her thinking as it was possible to be.

There was a red lever under the floor in the bottom of the craft which when pulled in an emergency caused it to jettison its floats and gear and shoot to the surface. It was not a joyride. The *Nautile* could get trapped. It could break. If it did, she thought, she would be lifted up by the flooding water and banged around at the top of the sphere. The cold would trigger in her the same mammalian diving reflex found in seals. Her heart would slow, blood would pour into the thoracic cavity to prevent her lungs collapsing, and the instinct to open her mouth and breathe would be more than the certain knowledge that doing so meant death. She would open and her larynx would constrict. Her nose and throat would be filled with water. The laryngospasm would not relax. Her lungs would be sealed off, and she would die a dry drowning by acidosis and hypoxia, head thrown back, eyes glassy and fearful like a doll's.

Saif got into the habit of laying down next to James in the evenings and talking at him. The most eloquent aside he made was about the plans to build the tallest building in the world in Jeddah.

166

'Have you been to New York?'

'Yes,' James said.

'This will be better. Twice the height of the Twin Towers! It will be a purity never seen before. Islam and the future will mix up in the sky. The lifts will play religious verse. You can be on the ground floor and watch the sun setting and then take a lift to the top and watch it set again.'

Mostly, Saif preached martyrdom. 'I expect to die soon,' he said, sucking on a mango skin. 'I welcome it. I expect you'll be killed too.' Saif turned to him. 'That is why I want you to convert to Islam.'

'No,' James said, firmly.

There was no chance he would convert. It was not just a question of Islam, it was the way life was constructed. A man lived his threescore years and ten, less than a whale, less than a roughy fish, and the only way to come to terms with his mortality was to partake in something that would outlive him; a field cleared of stones, a piece of jewellery, a monument, a machine. Every man was a loyalist for what he knew. Even tramps fought for the tramping life. Life was too short for him to renounce the English parish church, once Catholic, with their knights' tombs, prayer cushions, flower arrangements, the brass lectern in the shape of an eagle. No, the quiet of those places – the ancient front door, the graveyard, the meadow, the damp – gave him a sense of belonging. He was loyal to them. It was too late to abandon the English canon, from Chaucer to Dickens, the First World War poets, Graham Greene typing through the smog and drizzle . . . He had said it before: he was an intelligence officer who reached out, spoke Arabic, read widely, but if the Crusades were invoked – and Saif was invoking them – then he was a Crusader. If he had to die at the hands of fanatics, he wished to remain familiar and coherent to those whom he loved and who loved him.

*

167

There existed around them a closeness of birds and silver bars of tarpon fish and elephants at their crossing. The tides turned. If you were lucky, the rain fell. It was very green. The question of paradise presented itself. Saif did not speak of the intercourse with houris due to those who were martyred in Ramadan (to which he was entitled), but of the many nightingales that were in paradise, the scented flowers, the lawns stretching away. It was Persian and unconvincingly iridescent, and more so coming from a Saudi who knew of gardens only as the strips of grass at the back of hotels and office blocks in Jeddah and Riyadh which were watered with treated sewage before dawn. Saif, the lion, had been happier in the wadi, eating camel meat, because the life there was closer to the steady state universe of prayer mat and sand, and the heating up and cooling down of days.

English Catholics often regard Foxe's *Book of Martyrs* as Protestant propaganda. Some may even agree with a Jesuit view at the time which held it to be 'a huge dunghill of your stinking martyrs'.

Foxe was a fanatic, yet also a kindly and gentle man, a good friend, by many accounts. He was tutor to the children of Henry Howard, Earl of Surrey, who was executed for treason in 1547. Among those children were Thomas, 4th Duke of Norfolk; Jane, Countess of Westmoreland; Henry, Earl of Northampton and their cousin Charles, commander of the English fleet against the Spanish Armada. Despite his close connection with the Catholic Howards, Foxe was involved in suppressing the cult of the Virgin Mary. He escaped from England during the reign of the Catholic Queen, Mary Tudor, and lived in poverty among the Protestants in Antwerp, Rotterdam, and Frankfurt. He wrote his first account of Christian martyrs in Geneva, with particular attention to the Protestant martyrs, and returned to England when Elizabeth took the throne. The cathedrals and all the wealthy churches purchased a copy of the book, as did every bishop and vaulting churchman. Foxe became a literary celebrity. Later editions of the *Book of Martyrs* ran to thousands of pages and listed the death sequence of each martyr with formality and a level of detail no jihadist will ever match. Indeed, if the standard of martyrology is set by the dim standards of al-Qaeda, Foxe could by comparison be held up as a trustworthy historian.

He was an English Catholic, far removed from Saif's gap-toothed insistence. He was descended from St Thomas More and, on his mother's side, from the Blessed William Howard, who was executed in Titus Oate's Popish Plot and beatified by Pope Pius XI. He revered Donne, read the republican Milton, and celebrated his recusant ancestors and the whaling captains who followed, also lawyers, farmers, priests and vicars, Jesuits who worked on the English Mission and who were buried in Rome, many Benedictine nuns who entered the convents in Leuven and Cambrai, colonial officers, newspapermen, spies for Rome, and spies for London; his father was Thomas More XVI.

God help him. He was a pocket of moisture, emptying into the sand.

He wanted to make a run for it like the French security officer in Mogadishu, who tiptoed away from his captors while they slept, and escaped barefoot through the streets of the shattered city at night, making it after several hours to the safety of Villa Somalia, which serves as the Presidential Palace of the Somali Transitional Government.

England had lost him, Britain had. Everything was green above and around him, but it was no paradise. The quarrel of leaves, vines, sloughs and quicksand brought him back to the comics he had read as a boy, which often dealt with the fight against the Japanese in Burma in the Second World War. The Japanese wore thick glasses, always squinted, and paced through the jungle with their bayonets attached, like insects, until there was a shout of 'Tommy let them have it!' in the caption box and the British and the Americans fired and those Nips, as the comic had it, exploded backwards with a resounding *aieeee!* Aieeee: a word which as a boy he thought was Japanese.

The American naval base at Manda Bay was even closer than Lamu. A few hours by speedboat. Hidden inside, he knew, was a helipad and huts belonging to a covert unit which flew SEALS and other specialised personnel into Somalia after an air strike on the enemy. The unit was charged with proof of kill: getting DNA samples from corpses after an air strike.

The sky could always open up. In 2010, one of the leading al-Qaeda commanders, Saleh Ali Nabhan, was killed by an American missile. He had been travelling in a convoy on a coastal road between Mogadishu and Kismayo. A few minutes after the kill the men from Manda Bay rappelled down from helicopters. Grazing Somalia only with their boots, not ever unclipping their harnesses, they zipped Nabhan's corpse and another into body bags, and took them up into the helicopters.

It was macabre how many fingers and parts of Muslim martyrs the United States of America had held on to. They were frozen solid and given a number. Who knew where these relics were stored, or for how long, or if a Muslim chaplain was ever brought to pray over them?

There was no way for him to signal the Americans. The camp was undetectable by satellite, unless you had an idea where to look. Even if they found it, it would be almost impossible for them to kill the holy warriors and save him alone.

There were prayer beads, sweat, raindrops. The men sat cross-legged on the sheeting. In their disillusionment talk of battles increased. He was raised to be merciful, but combat always reverted to blockbuster

170

action. His captors deserved to die. Let them be martyrs. It was important to kill them before they launched another attack on innocents as they had in Kampala in 2010. The jihad could not win.

Say it did. The caliphate would have its own power structures and careerists. Everything would be scrubbed with cheap soap. Women would be hooded and put in their place. Macroeconomics would be beyond such a regime. Organised crime would flourish because the clerics have no idea how to deal with pornography, gambling and drug addiction other than by public beating and execution.

He read the jihadist literature. He respectfully spoke the words aloud. The Arabic was powerful, but his mind was settled on other books. He preferred Bacon's *New Atlantis* to More's *Utopia*. He had read it again and again. The first time had been by chance, in the army. It comforted him nearly as much as the rosary he recited for protection: it propounded a celebration of a society organised around the pursuit of knowledge and the duty of compassion.

He placed himself once more on the ship which in 1623 sailed from Peru bound for Japan. The vessel lost its way in the unexplored vastness of the Pacific. The sailors were without victuals and were preparing themselves for death when they spotted land on the horizon: New Atlantis. Drawing close they were amazed to see it was not a squalid atoll, but an island with the low and certain boscage of a northern country – a Gotland or an Anglesey. They sailed into the harbour of the capital, Bensalem, a small town, finely built in a style reminiscent of Dalmatia and manorial Somerset, and were met in cordial order by a man in a headscarf more daintily made than a Turkish turban. This Oriental personage, with hair falling down from under the fabric, with the aspect of a gentle Sufi, was a Christian. New Atlantis had been converted to Christianity at a very early date through the miracle of a cedar ark which had sunk in the Mediterranean Sea, travelled improbably on the currents, and bobbed up not far from New Atlantis. There was an orb of light over it and when a theatre of boats

171

approached, it broke apart to reveal a pillar of light, 'not sharp, but in form of a column, or cylinder, rising from the sea a great way up towards heaven; and at the top of it was seen a large cross of light, more bright and resplendent than the body of the pillar'.

While their ship was repaired and provisioned, the sailors were taken ashore and accommodated in rich lodgings. After some weeks of recuperation they were given a tour of New Atlantis, with great care taken that they kept their distance from the New Atlanteans in the outlying towns.

New Atlantis was a country in which the guilds and the church, the farmers and the traders, were happily married. In its hills were caves with pits. Scientists were lowered to the bottom on ropes and there coagulated, indurated and refrigerated materials. Hermits sat apart in the same blackness, without candles. Atop the hills were towers of stone and wood for the observation of meteors, lightning, wind, snow and hail.

The New Atlanteans studied nature and imitated it. They developed flying machines and glided off hills and had 'ships and boats for going underwater, and brooking of seas'.

In the towns were institutions that resembled the modern research university. These places of invention brought forth gyroscopes such as were later developed for nuclear submarines and 'divers curious clocks and other like motions of return', all of them 'strange for equality, fine-ness, and subtlety'. The inventors, scientists, mystery men – the traders of illumination and timekeeping – all processed through the towns. The best of those who had advanced the cause of knowledge were immor-talised in a hall of statues, 'some of brass; some of marble and touchstone; some of cedar and other special woods gilt and adorned; some of iron; some of silver; some of gold'.

Often in his despond he sat himself down in a cool part of the inven-tor's hall in New Atlantis. It stood oblique from the twenty-first century jihadist camp, yet was connected in his mind, as he supposed the jinn cities were connected in the minds of some Muslims, as Danny's undersea world was not yet connected. The hall was of the highest quality brickwork – red, Venetian – and the light slanted down through the high windows in a different way to the light through the windows in the rooms frequented by Yusuf al-Afghani.

If he could remain in the inventor's hall he would be gathered up by the New Atlanteans and cured with kindness. His health would recover, and he would be shown other curiosities, perhaps a clockwork dove that when wound up flew the length of a pasture and returned with each beat of a wooden wing, slower, slower, and deeper, apparently tired, and came to rest again in his hand.

It was clear to him. Religious authority would not stand a chance once it had to confront the issue of species survival. There would be a shift in morality from goodness to necessity. Islam and Evangelical Christianity would lose their dominion as quickly as the Roman Catholic Church did in Quebec in 1968. What could be accomplished by a Last Judgement the governments of the fascist future would not themselves accomplish? New cults concerned with the harvesting of body parts and brains, he believed, would absorb the mystical agency of angels, demons, miracles and creation myths. Religious belief would be reduced to its most sensible parts.

Politically, the jihad would become outworn, its arguments and methods a sideshow, agitators among other agitators, as in the dying days of anarchism.

In tennis, the future decided the past: where the racquet ends up influences where the ball goes. Everything depended on the follow-through. There was no follow-through in modern politics. You could see that in the failure of politicians to grasp the nettle on climate change and in the talk of philosophers about wasted lives.

173

The thousands of illegal migrants who journey by sea, he was certain, would turn into millions. When the vessels and rafts were turned back, rammed, sunk, as they inevitably would be, authoritarianism would follow. There would be race riots again. The walls were already being built higher and into a maze. He was one of those laying the bricks. He had seen it in the British embassies in Africa, where the new rule was that an African seeking a visa to enter the United Kingdom could only meet with a clerical officer of local nationality – a pseudo-Roman – and never with a British consular officer.

Of course none of this touched on Danny's question of a reboot of mankind, where the genetic distinctiveness of human beings breaks down.

One characteristic of sea creatures is their constant movement. Not grief, not anything can stop them. A tuna tagged off Martinique recently was caught fifty days later in Breisundet in Norway, near the fishing town of Ålesund.

The Cuvier's beaked whale dives, touches the ligament of the sea's throat, and rises again. It breaks for breath in the light, then returns to the deep. Whereas Christ, after his Crucifixion, continued up from hell through all the visible and invisible heavens to the highest dwelling place of God.

The Latin term for the feast of ascension is ascencio, which describes how Christ was supposed to have lifted off from the earth under his own power, leaving the mark of his foot in the rock.

She took with her a pocket calculator, a digital camera, a notebook, soft lead pencils, a thermos of coffee and a packed lunch of bread, cheese and salami bought from the supermarket in Iceland. Thumbs gave her a music compilation to play on the craft.

It was a clear morning. The sea was calm. The pilot climbed in first, then the other scientist, then her. Two men, one woman. She wore the same running shoes she used for the treadmill. She went up the ladder and dropped down through the hatch. It was a thick nickel sphere. There was no need for decompression: the pressure inside was a constant one atmosphere. The walls were covered in dials and switches. There were three viewing windows and three padded benches. The smell was of bleach and behind it of sick. The carpet was very thin, brown, shiny; of the kind you might find in the entrance to a prison or a military installation. She put on her ski hat. The hatch was closed above them and sealed.

The *Nautile* was winched down over the side and into the Greenland Sea. There was a clanging of chains, final checks, and then they sank. The colours coming into the craft changed like the colour of the sky seen by a rocket when it blasts into space, although of a different density: school ink, blue, blue-black, black. She saw charr, starfish and little whirring shrimps. The craft began to breathe. Oxygen was pumped in and the carbon dioxide they expelled was scrubbed clean by a lithium-hydroxide filter. The biggest window was for the pilot. Her window was the size of a laptop screen. She pressed her face to the thick quartz pane. She wanted to feel the trembling on the other side. She could not see much, the monitors from the cameras were a truer guide. Even so it was important to look with her own eyes. She gazed into the deep and the deep gazed back.

Nuclear submarines went windowless in the wristwatch shallows, without a care to look out – only listening, making no sound. A submersible was just the opposite. It was a seeing device: from the *Nautile* people had observed the hull of the *Titanic*.

*

'Come on, Danny, just play the music,' said Peter, the German scientist.

'It's Tom's usual rubbish,' she protested.

'We have a whole day together,' pointed out Étienne, the pilot.

So she gave up Thumbs's compilation. The lyrics of the first track reverberated: *I travel the world and the seven seas*.

Étienne touched the stern thrusters. They sank, sank, sank. All the waters closed over their heads: 607 metres . . . 634 metres . . . out of the mesopelagic layer . . . into the bathypelagic. There was a time when the dominion of countries ended at five fathoms, the keel of a ship, the run of an anchor. Enki was at 3133 metres, 1741 fathoms.

The sphere was too small to stand up in; after an hour, her legs became numb. She wiped away their condensed breath from the window and stared out. There was another hour of descent to go.

'Étienne, could you turn off the lights?' Peter asked.

'All of them?'

'Yes, please.'

Everything that belonged to them disappeared, except the light on the switches and on the emergency lever. The water was alive with bioluminescent fish and eels. The salp and jellyfish gave themselves in disco lights when the *Nautile* brushed them. Down there everything spoke in light: it was the most common form of communication on the planet. The puniest fish had the brightest lanterns. There were fish who wore a cape of silver chain mail to reflect light. Transparency was another form of protection. So was casting a red light to appear black and so invisible. Or to fill one's belly with ink and so disappear, as surely as slipping on a magic ring.

There was a slowness at that depth which matched the Ray Charles song that was playing. *Here we go again, she's back in town again.*

'That's you, Danny,' said Peter.

'You wish.'

The darkness was so strong it bent her memory of summer twilight in London.

They sank deeper.

'Can we turn up the lights now?' Peter asked.

'Certainly,' said Étienne.

Everything was illuminated. The gold dolphin badge on Étienne's beanie shone.

The sphere creaked. The microphones picked up ghostly whining, knocks, moaning, shrieks, wailing, and firing. The walls grew cold. They were wet to the touch. She began to smell the men; they might have begun to smell her. She wiped away more condensation from the porthole with her elbow; 921 metres . . . 1043 metres.

'Starboard. Jewelled squid!' exclaimed Peter.

They hovered to get a better look. She zoomed in with the video camera.

'You're right,' she conceded.

The squid were white and appeared to be encrusted with emeralds and amethysts. They had a massive sapphire eye for looking about them and a tiny eye pushed into their bodies like genitalia. They swam at a 45-degree angle to make use of both eyes.

Peter was wiry, with frizzy hair; an environmental activist. Étienne was more classical, with a Roman nose, very precise; a sacristan, delighted with life, or himself.

Peter was talking about whales falling. He had a strong German accent. His voice was high-pitched.

'I mean, can you imagine seeing a dead whale dropping past our window. It comes down sharply, like so.' He demonstrated. 'What a feast for those at the bottom! Just think of the weight in worms and lice in the stomach.'

1830 metres . . . 1832 metres. They were covered up. All of Britain could be sunk over them, the peak of Ben Nevis would not see any trace of daylight.

There were strings of bell-jar jellies with numerous transparent stomachs, all of them pulsing. The ocean was hungry. It was a mouth, and a grave.

A beaked whale has a heart attack in the Ligurian Sea and dies. It sinks and its head is mashed on the sides of an underground canyon. Immediately its cheeks are flushed with bacteria. There are worms, spider crabs and all manner of creatures feeding on a single vertebra. Gulper eels eat their body weight in a minute, then go without for weeks. Anglerfish cloak themselves so that their scales are like the glowing excrement of marine snow. Another fish tries to eat the excrement and the anglerfish opens its fanged mouth.

There was a fish with an eye covering half of its head. She saw a fish with a deathly pallor whose face was like a sponge with holes pushed into it by a pencil. Each of those holes was a sensory pore detecting the slightest movement nearby.

The *Nautile* stopped in a cold layer of the water. It keeled over, righted itself, shuddered, and continued to sink. The thermal layers were like a staircase going down. She said thermal layer and a lithograph presented itself of her slave ship halted on such a layer, not able to sink any deeper, instead carried forever on the North Atlantic Drift, its fire doused, its souls intact, in irons, their lungs full of water.

'It's scary,' Peter said. They were talking about the deep. 'I mean, there's a reason hell is down there. There's a reason heaven is up there. It's conditioned by evolution.'

Étienne believed that, in geological terms, man was going to be a short-lived species. 'We are poisonous. We are quick. We are the noodles of evolution.'

'Instant noodles,' she said. If the world kept spinning, if the waters held in, the deep would be constant until the end of geological time. Instantly made, instantly gone. If man had a sense of proportion, he would die of shame. His salvation was that he lived in denial. She had

178

not given up, but it was in the balance. *Homo sapiens* was either at the start of a very long journey, or close to the end of a very short one. If it was to be an odyssey, the history which had passed since Sumer would come to seem priceless and savage. If it was to be a short venture, man's mark would be the rubbish he had buried in the ground.

'Even eating our way through cows, apples, everything, in our billions, you know we're nothing compared to the life down there. That life can't be destroyed, it feeds on death – or less than death – it reconfigures and goes further in, into hotter water.'

A lot will depend on the ability of scientists to manipulate microbial life, so that in the future it can be trowelled into the grooves on an irradiated orb and animate life there. Once we learn how to throw a dome over the rock and calibrate gravity so that it does not stretch or wither us, make us sick, dull or depressed, then the animated moon can serve as a vessel. It will sit at the centre of a Saturn-sized ball of water and cruise through space, encased, a miniature Abzu, a marble within a marble.

The new world's challenges will be similar to those at the bottom of the sea: how to avoid predators, how to eat and how to find a mate.

It is understandable you would want to come back as yourself into a wonderland with the sharpness of colour of the Queen of Hearts in a newly opened pack of cards. But coming back as yourself is resurrection. It is uncommon. It may even be greater than the scope of mathematics.

We cannot talk with definition about our souls, but it is certain that we will decompose. Some dust of our bodies may end up in a horse, wasp, cockerel, frog, flower or leaf, but for every one of these sensational assemblies there are a quintillion microorganisms. It is far likelier that the greater part of us will become protists than a skyscraping dormouse. What is likely is that, sooner or later, carried in the wind and in rivers, or your graveyard engulfed in the sea, a portion of each of us will be given new life in the cracks, vents, or pools of molten sulphur on which the tongue fish skate.

You will be in Hades, the staying place of the spirits of the dead. You will be drowned in oblivion, the River Lethe, swallowing water to erase all memory. It will not be the nourishing womb you began your life in. It will be a submergence. You will take your place in the boiling-hot fissures, among the teeming hordes of nameless micro-organisms that mimic no forms, because they are the foundation of all forms. In your reanimation you will be aware only that you are a fragment of what once was, and are no longer dead. Sometimes this will be an electric feeling, sometimes a sensation of the acid you eat, or the furnace under you. You will burgle and rape other cells in the dark for a seeming eternity, but nothing will come of it. Hades is evolved to the highest state of simplicity. It is stable. Whereas you are a tottering tower, so young in evolutionary terms, and addicted to consciousness.

He had watched lambs gambol on the hill by the jinn pit. It would be an ecological future, where even the gas from cremations would be captured for power generation. Yet his experience in Somalia — with darkness and deprivation, the famished condition of the Somali people, the desolation of the wadi, his clashing on behalf of the Enlightenment (so he persuaded himself) — would look like a buccaneering life to many in that future, to be envied above a world in which every infant was to be registered at birth and tracked with implants drilled into bone.

In another of the letters Danny had written him, she had reported the unexpected pleasure of looking after a dog for a friend; taking the dog for walks, brushing its coat, trying to read its expressions in the evening, before moving continuously into thoughts about the new human beings that will be available within a few decades:

I wonder if we'll have anything of Jenny in us. Her eyes, her wagging tail, her eagerness to please. Probably not. We'll get new muscle and ligaments, new skin, new eyes and ears. What's the Olympic motto? Faster, higher, stronger? It's predatory. We'll go for snakes, hawks and sharks. Some of it will be messing about with genes, splicing, but a lot is going to be technology. A metal exoskeleton, I should think. More bounce, better protection. We might find a way to link human memories to a mainframe . . .

The letter ventured off into talk of the town and holiday plans, then circled back.

People who say no to upgrades will end up in caravan parks and wild places. They will become slower and weaker relative to the others. In time they will turn into curiosities, human beasts, until curiosity dies like it did for Kafka's hunger artist, who fasted to death in a cage and was replaced with a panther.

His brain was white stuff: spermaceti, galantine. The shapes that played on the inside of his eyelids were vivid, and when he retreated further into New Atlantis he saw the important horse race of the season was run on a course very like the racecourse in his town in northern England – a flat race that had been run since the reign of King George III – he sensed that the place names of the villages in New Atlantis were Anglo-Saxon, and that this was natural, because the Angles and Saxons came from a landscape that was similar to that remote island — their language was sensitive to dips in the land, the culvert under a hill, the slopes and mounds, there were leas, dales, holts, slades and wolds in New Atlantis, as there were in England. Somalis must have similar words. The land he passed over on the lorry had glowered; it was waterless, unmarked and unnamed to him, just the wadis, the companionless trees, and the shadows in the cuts of the badlands.

There were days when the wind blew hard before the rain and he had to anchor his net with rocks. The creek turned to jade, crabs scuttled in greater numbers on the banks of putty mud from one settlement to another. The tide rose, and there was gunfire and shouting in the forest.

Almost all of his sober passages of thought involved people long ago dead. He wished he was in England, following the edges of a wood . . . God, enough. He wished he was with her. That was all. It didn't matter where. It had been his training to push away thoughts of what might be but now he was in the place of martyrs and he was slipping away and there was no more space for death, there was only space for life, for her. She was so beautiful, to him, so strong, so true. He wanted more than anything to hold her. He could feel the embrace; her shirt, her shoulders, his head on her shoulder, her hands cradling him; him sobbing into her, crying the way you do in dreams, without any inhibition. He had recreated every word, every experience of her; tried to understand it. And the joy; the joy was that he was not making it up. She felt the same way. She said so in the letters she had sent him, always physical letters, handwritten, so he could never be at liberty to file her away, she said, or share her on a screen.

But death is remorseless. Death is the tide which sweeps away conscious-ness. It is the absolute zero which stops any acceleration. Poetry speaks of the ocean as a tomb, whereas science reckons it to be a womb. If you must waste away or perish violently in the morning light then a burial at sea might resolve this conflicted view. Lash me in a hammock and drop me deep . . . Would you wish to be sunk to a great depth, or to be dropped a fathom down, on a reef, gently rocked, until your bones are of corals made and you suffer a sea change into something rich and strange?

A year or so before – it seemed a lifetime ago – he had been at a dinner party on a farm not far from Mount Kenya. It was well attended, very smart, but the mood was subdued: a European royal who had been a close friend to the hosts lay gravely ill in his palace overlooking the North Sea. This royal had promised – extravagantly or on a Jungian impulse – that were it possible, his soul would take the form of a daemon at the time of his passing and appear to his friends. During the main course, a bird with carmine breast feathers appeared on the veranda. No one at the table had seen such a bird before. It was remarked upon. The bird did not settle in the thatched roof with the weaverbirds, but sat forthrightly on a vase in front of the hostess. It looked at her, cocking its head to one side in the way birds do, then it hopped around and regarded the others at the table.

'My God, it's Bernhard,' the hostess said.

Everyone fell silent.

'Bernhard!' she called out, at which the bird warbled, bowed, and flew off.

'Excuse me,' the hostess said, 'I must call Europe.'

Sure enough, she was informed that the prince had died a few minutes before.

What form might he take in death? If he could appear to Danny, he would be a small African owl, fluttering at her porthole. If he could only send a message, some sign of the afterlife, he would return to her the inscription she had written inside the cover of one of his books, from Job:

> Have you entered the springs of the sea? Or have you walked in the depths? Have the gates of death been revealed to you? Or have you seen the door of the shadow of death? Have you comprehended the breadth of the Earth? Tell me if you know all this?

He would have messages for his family and friends, but the passage from Job would be his sign to her.

The Kaaba was the empty space to which all Muslims directed their prayers. He was sceptical – Catholic, English, he desired a New Atlantis, a windswept All Souls College – still the Kaaba caused him to shudder. If he were allowed a supernatural instruction, it would be for her to achieve a dispensation to study the microbial life inside it.

He was standing in the creek washing himself. Ablution, with no rhythm, no conviction. He saw it coming a few seconds before it hit. The colours on its snub nose were the same maroon as the flashes 1 Para wore on their right arm. It was his colour. It was coming for him.

How it twirled towards the ground. He was transfixed. He thought of a helter-skelter, circling down on hessian mats heavy with sand, those colours going round and round, 'Helter Skelter, feare no colours, course him, trounce him!'

It glinted. It burned from its tail. It was an astonishing creation. Entirely human, wholly American. It had been fired over the curvature of the earth from a submarine off the coast of Somalia. The viscosity of seawater at so many fathoms, the loosening of rocket motors in flight, the load of explosives, the Coriolis effect as it applied at the

184

equator, all of these considerations had been accounted for by minds and machines, yet it was impossible in the final moment not to see the missile as something more.

Machine guns were fired.

'I'm bleeding out,' someone cried in Arabic.

'*Allah u Akbar!*' was the last utterance heard.

He dived into the creek. With all his strength, he kicked to the bottom. Addition, subtraction. His mind stopped like a roulette wheel. His last thought, peculiarly, blessedly, was of the wool markets in Langland's *Piers the Ploughman*. The wine merchant calling out 'Wine from Alsace! Wine from Gascony! Rhine wines!'

The surface exploded like a star. The sides of the creek were thrown up into the sky. The noise was so loud it became silence. Then there was that secondary platinum light that turns bodies to ash.

The sun went so fast, the stars faster, yet not as fast as young More's body to the earth. He came up for air in bloody gaining waters, with cooked crabs, with martyrs. He looked at death, went under again, and swam away, towards the Boni, towards Kenya. In this sense, at least, his submergence was shallow.

3088 metres . . . 3120 . . .

'There it is now, Danny,' Étienne said, with feeling. 'Your Enki.' They went slowly towards a column the size of an office block. The chimneys on it billowed like so many Turks setting back their heads and expelling cigarette smoke through their nostrils.

It was in the style of Gaudi; pitted, knobbly, rust-coloured from oxidation, black in places, in others mottled white with mats of bacteria. Amphipod danced at the edge of the vents. Tubeworms swayed like heavy cocks. There were mussels and other bivalves. Blind fish circled. The Turks sat very still, smoking, regarding them.

After some time at the base of the column Étienne lifted the *Nautile* and piloted it to where the floor of the earth was cracked. There was no fire, no hearth. The magma was glassy and cool. The light broke against heavy drifts of marine snow; it was useless to think the abyss could be illuminated by thallium iodide. She was excited, intent, but at the same time thought, the places we will have to dwell as a species are terrible. We will have to accommodate ourselves to realms for which we are not evolved, to lodge ourselves in them, to articulate our bodies from inside a suit of titanium and the other materials. She felt the metal hollow inside the submersible acutely – the stale air, the sweat of Peter and Étienne, the smell of vomit, bleach . . .

With great care Étienne set the *Nautile* down at the edge of a crack. They extended the robot arm to scrape bacteria from its interior. She adjusted her weight on the bench and the craft in turn settled on the fine silica mud, on the diatomaceous ooze of dead creatures that on land was used as scouring powder.

Étienne turned off the spotlights.

'Testing systems.'

They did not speak. There was just the sound of their breathing. She touched her forehead to the quartz. Outside, viscous black flowed into black. My God, it was a trance, it was the most consuming painting. A powerful sense of vertigo overcame her, of a kind she had not experienced since the day she tried to follow James into the wood on the grounds of the Hotel Atlantic. She felt the *Nautile* was too close to the edge, that they were teetering, and would fall into the underworld, the true under-world. She felt that the *Nautile* would break apart, the three of them would fall out, and she herself would tumble down, like Alice, but not into Wonderland. Her body would be a puff of life, gone, instantly, with no possibility of ascent, and the same for Peter and Étienne; each of them cartwheeling into a chemical soup.

You lift off to heaven, you sink into hell. You rocket into space, you drown on a slave ship. The encompassing sea of Abzu made more

186

sense than any astral plane put forward by the great religions. Why not a sea behind the universe, making fast the stars?

She admired the musculature of ballet dancers, but understood that they were liquid beings, trailing tendril lives. The gas bladders of fish burst and filled their mouths when the net was winched up. Salp lost structure, died and became indefinable at the surface. All living crea-tures were at some point disassembled. It was only a question of where the parts ended up and were made into something new. The volume of life in the deep, its complexity and self-organisation, would over millions of years take in the disassembled from the land as it crumbled into the sea and was washed away by rivers and rains. It was too dramatic to say damned souls cooked in agony while satanic whores scored them with fingernails and others with flaccid and scaly bodies dashed them against the shiny obsidian . . .

It was tranquil, in a way. There were no storms, no swells, the water was very calm. Did the abyss sing of itself? Seen from below, the surface looked like heaven. Seen from heaven, she thought, it was a roiling sea, a darksome air infernal. Human beings were between worlds, they were inbetweeners, who did not know where light dwelt or where darkness had its place.

Her eyes adjusted. There were again the soft glowing switches, like the smoking signs on old airliners at night; the association with seamless life, the comfort of collective awareness, common nostalgia. She could make out Étienne, leaning forward. Her sense of vertigo left her. She felt that she more clearly belonged to the present.

'All right,' said Étienne. 'Let's take her up.'

Another epitaph would be from the Roman poet Horace:
'Plunge it in deep water: it comes up more beautiful.'

ACKNOWLEDGEMENTS

I would like to remember:
The French DSGE secret agent Dennis Allex, who was captured by an al-Qaeda-linked faction of the Shabab in Mogadishu on 14 July 2009. At the time of writing he is still being held hostage.

The hundreds of sailors and yachtsmen captured at sea by Somali pirates and held at gunpoint off the coast of Somalia.

Asho Duhulow, who was stoned to death in Kismayo on 27 October 2008. She was thirteen years old.

Thanks to:
The Woods Hole Oceanographic Institution, Columbia University and ETH Zurich, whose scientists patiently and brilliantly introduced me to the world of oceanography.

My friends in the mighty nation of Somalia, who welcomed me in a time of distress.

The Economist, for allowing me to follow the story.

The Tasmanian Writers Centre, for generously providing space to write.

191